We slid out—stooped down, not breathing, and not making the least noise.

We sneaked towards the fence and got to it all right. Jim and me went over it, but Tom's pants catched on a splinter on the top rail. We heard steps coming, so Tom had to pull loose. That made the splinter snap. As Tom dropped alongside of Jim and me, somebody calls out, "Who's that? Answer, or I'll shoot!"

We didn't answer—just ran as fast as we could. There was a rush and a bang, bang, bang! Bullets whizzed around us.

We heard the men yell, "There they are! They're headed for the river! After them, men!"

A Note about *Huckleberry Finn*

Huckleberry Finn takes place around 1845, along the Mississippi River from Missouri down to Arkansas. The characters express themselves in various dialects, the customary speech of their time, region, and social group.

Huck, a poor, uneducated white boy, speaks and writes in a Southern dialect marked by numerous grammar and spelling errors: *that ain't no matter*; *I says*; *intellectural*. Jim, a black man who has spent his life in slavery, speaks in what Mark Twain called "Missouri Negro dialect," which deviates even further from standard English. For example, Jim's dialect includes dropped final letters, the substitution of *d* for *th*, and omitted or incorrect verbs: *I's still yo' fren*; *Dat's good*; *Who dere?*

Huckleberry Finn is widely regarded as a masterpiece partly because of its linguistic realism. When the book appeared in 1885, this realism was groundbreaking; many found it coarse and shocking. Even today the book's language is controversial. In particular, many readers take offense at the characters' use of the term *nigger*. In Huck's day, however, *nigger* was common dialect for *Negro*, especially among the uneducated.

The voices of *Huckleberry Finn* are the voices that Twain heard when he was growing up. Huck, the narrator, has such an authentic voice that he seems present, speaking directly to us. To read the book is to listen to Huck, and others, *talk*.

MARK TWAIN

The Adventures of
HUCKLEBERRY
FINN

Edited, and with an Afterword,
by Joan Dunayer

 THE TOWNSEND LIBRARY

THE ADVENTURES OF HUCKLEBERRY FINN

TP THE TOWNSEND LIBRARY

For more titles in the Townsend Library,
visit our website: **www.townsendpress.com**

All new material in this edition is
copyright © 2004 by Townsend Press.
Printed in the United States of America

0 9 8 7 6 5 4 3

Illustrations © 2004 by Hal Taylor

Townsend Press, Inc.
439 Kelley Drive
West Berlin, New Jersey 08091
cs@townsendpress.com

ISBN-13: 978-1-59194-029-6
ISBN-10: 1-59194-029-X

Library of Congress Control Number:
2004104206

TABLE OF CONTENTS

AFTERWORD

Chapter 1

You don't know about me without you have read a book by the name of *The Adventures of Tom Sawyer*. But that ain't no matter. That book was made by Mr. Mark Twain, and he told the truth, mainly. There was things that he stretched, but that's nothing: I never seen anybody but lied one time or another, without it was Tom's Aunt Polly, or the Widow Douglas, or maybe Mary, who all is told about in that book.

The way that book winds up is this: Tom and me found the money that the robbers hid in the cave, and it made us rich. We got six thousand dollars apiece—all gold. It was an awful sight of money when it was piled up. Judge Thatcher took it and put it out at interest, and it fetched us a dollar a day apiece all year 'round—more than a body could tell what to do with.

The Widow Douglas took me for her son and planned to civilize me, but it was rough living in the house all the time, considering how dismal regular and decent the widow was in all her ways. So when I couldn't stand it no more, I lit out. I got back into my old rags, slept in my sugar barrel, and was free and satisfied. But Tom Sawyer hunted me up and said he was going to start a band of robbers, and I could join if I'd go back to the widow and be respectable. So I went back.

The widow cried over me and called me a poor lost lamb. She put me in new clothes again, and I couldn't do nothing but sweat and feel all cramped up. Then the old thing began again. The widow rung a bell for supper, and I had to come right away. When I got to the table, I couldn't go right to eating but had to wait for the widow to tuck down her head and grumble a little over the food, though there warn't anything the matter with it—that is, nothing except that everything was cooked by itself. In a barrel of odds and ends, it's different; things get mixed up, and the juice kind of swaps around, and the things taste better.

After supper the widow got out her Bible and learned me about Moses. At first I was all in a sweat to find out about him. But by and by she said that Moses had been dead a long time. Then I didn't care about him no more because I don't take no stock in dead people.

Pretty soon I wanted to smoke and asked the widow to let me. She wouldn't. She said it was a nasty practice and wasn't clean, and I mustn't do it anymore. That's just the way with some people.

They get down on a thing when they don't know nothing about it. Here she was bothering about Moses, who was no kin to her, and no use to anybody—being gone, you see—yet finding fault with me for doing a thing that had some good in it. The widow took snuff. Of course, *that* was all right because she done it herself.

The widow's sister, Miss Watson, a skinny old maid with eyeglasses, come to live with the widow. She set to learning me to spell. She worked me hard for about an hour. Then the widow made her ease up. I couldn't 've stood it much longer. Then for an hour it was deadly dull, and I was fidgety. Miss Watson said, "Don't put your feet up there, Huckleberry. Don't scrunch up like that, Huckleberry. Set up straight. Don't yawn and stretch like that, Huckleberry. Why don't you try to behave?"

Miss Watson told me all about Hell, and I said I wished I was there. She got mad then. But I didn't mean no harm. All I wanted was to go somewheres. I warn't particular. She said it was wicked to say what I said. She said *she* was going to live so that she'd go to Heaven. Well, I couldn't see no advantage in going where *she* was going, so I made up my mind I wouldn't try for it. Miss Watson told me all about Heaven. She said all a body had to do there was to go around all day with a harp and sing, forever. So I didn't think much of it. But I never said so. I asked Miss Watson if she reckoned Tom Sawyer would go to Heaven, and she said, "Not by a long sight!" I was glad about that because I wanted Tom and me to be together.

By and by, Miss Watson and the widow fetched the niggers* in and had prayers.

Then everybody was off to bed. I went up to my room with a piece of candle and put it on the table. I set down in a chair by the window and tried to think of something cheerful, but it warn't no use. I felt so lonesome that I almost wished I was dead. The stars was shining, and the leaves rustled in the woods ever so mournful. I heard an owl, a ways off, hoo-hooing about somebody that was dead, and a dog crying about somebody that was going to die. Away out in the woods I heard the sound that a ghost makes when it wants to tell about something that's on its mind but can't make itself understood, and so can't rest easy in its grave and has to go around every night grieving. I got so downhearted and scared that I did wish I had some company. I got out my pipe for a smoke 'cause the widow wouldn't know.

After a long time, I heard the clock away off in the town go "boom" twelve times. Then all was still again, stiller than ever.

Pretty soon I heard a twig snap down in the dark amongst the trees. Something was stirring. I

*Although the word "nigger" is insulting today, Huck does not intend it as a racist slur. In his day, uneducated people often used the term instead of "Negro."

set still and listened. Directly I could just barely hear "Meow, meow" down there. I says "Meow" as soft as I could, put out the light, and scrambled out of the window onto the shed. I slipped down to the ground and crawled in amongst the trees. There was Tom Sawyer waiting for me.

Tom and me tiptoed down a path towards the end of the widow's garden, stooping down so that the branches wouldn't scrape our heads. When we was passing the kitchen, I fell over a root and made a noise. We scrouched down and laid still.

Miss Watson's big nigger, Jim, was setting in the kitchen door. Tom and me could see him pretty clear because there was a light behind him. Jim got up and stretched his neck out a minute, listening. "Who dere?" He listened some more. Then he come down and stood right between Tom and me. We nearly could've touched him. "Who dere?" Jim says again. He set down on the ground between Tom and me, leaned his back against a tree, and stretched his legs out 'til one of them almost touched one of mine. My nose begun to itch. It itched 'til the tears come into my eyes. But I didn't dare scratch. This miserableness went on six or seven minutes, but it seemed longer than that. Then Jim begun to breathe heavy. Next he begun to snore.

Tom made a sign to me—a little noise with his mouth—and we went creeping away on our hands and knees. When we was ten foot off, Tom said he hadn't got enough candles; he would slip into the kitchen and get some more. I didn't want him to try. I said Jim might wake up. But Tom wanted to risk it. So we slid in there and got three candles. Tom laid five cents on the table as payment.

As soon as Tom was back, we headed to the steep hill on the other side of the house. When we got to the top, we looked down on the town and could see three or four lights twinkling. The stars over us was sparkling ever so fine. Down by the town was the Mississippi, a whole mile broad and awful still and grand.

We went down the hill and found Joe Harper and Ben Rogers hid in the old tannery. We unhitched a skiff and pulled down the river two and a half miles, to the big scar on the hillside, and went ashore.

We went to a clump of bushes. Tom made Joe and Ben swear to keep the secret and then showed them a hole in the hill, right in the thickest part of the bushes. We lit the candles and crawled in on our hands and knees. We went about two hundred yards. Then the cave opened up. Tom poked around amongst the passages. Pretty soon he ducked under a wall where you wouldn't 've noticed that there was a hole. We went along a narrow place and got into a kind of room, all damp and cold. We stopped there.

Tom says, "Now we'll start this band of robbers and call it Tom Sawyer's Gang. Everybody that wants to join has to take an oath and write his name in blood."

Everybody was willing.

Tom got out a sheet of paper that he had wrote the oath on and read it. It swore every boy to stick to the band and never tell any of its secrets. If anybody done anything to any boy in the band, whichever boy was ordered to kill that person must do it, and he mustn't eat or sleep 'til he killed them. If anybody that belonged to the band told the secrets, he must have his throat cut. His carcass would be burned and the ashes scattered all around. The gang would blot his name off of the list with blood, put a curse on it, and never mention it again.

Everybody said it was a real beautiful oath and asked Tom if he got it out of his own head. He said some of it, but the rest was out of books about pirates and robbers. He said that every high-toned gang had an oath.

Joe thought it would be good to kill the families of boys that told the secrets. Tom said that was a good idea, so he took a pencil and wrote it in.

Then Ben says, "Huck ain't got no family. What you going to do about *him*?"

"He's got a father," Tom says.

"Yes, he's got a father, but you can't never find him these days. He used to lay drunk with the hogs in the tannery, but he ain't been seen for a year or more."

I was glad that I hadn't seen Pap for more than a year. I didn't want to see him no more. He always hit me when he was sober and could get his hands on me. I took to the woods most of the time when he was around.

The boys talked it over. They was going to rule me out because every boy must have a family or somebody else to kill, or it wouldn't be fair. Nobody could think of anything to do. I was almost ready to cry when I thought of Miss Watson. I told them that they could kill *her*.

Everybody said, "She'll do. Huck can come in."

Then we all stuck a pin in our finger, to get blood to sign with, and signed the paper.

"Now," Ben says, "what's this gang's line of business?"

"Robbery and murder," Tom says.

"What are we going to rob—houses or cattle?"

"Stealing cattle and such things ain't robbery. It's burglary," Tom says. "We ain't burglars. That ain't no sort of style. We're highwaymen. We stop stagecoaches and carriages on the road, with masks on, and kill the people and take their watches and money."

"Must we always kill the people?" Joe says.

"Certainly. Some authorities think different, but mostly it's considered best to kill them— except some that you bring to the cave and keep here 'til people pay you money to set them free.

And you don't kill the women. You're always polite to them. By and by, they fall in love with you and never want to go home."

Tom said we'd meet again next week and rob somebody and kill some people. Ben said he couldn't get out much except for Sundays, so he wanted to begin next Sunday. But Tom and Joe said it would be wicked to do it on Sunday. We agreed to get together and fix a day as soon as we could. Then we elected Tom first captain and Joe second captain and started home.

I clumb up the shed and crept into my window just before daybreak. My new clothes was all dirty with grease and clay, and I was real tired.

In the morning I got a good scolding from Miss Watson on account of my clothes. The widow didn't scold; she just cleaned off the grease and clay and looked so sad that I thought I'd behave awhile if I could.

Miss Watson told me to pray every day, and I'd get whatever I asked for. But it warn't so. I tried it. Once I got a fishing line but no hooks. A fishing line warn't any good to me without hooks. I tried for the hooks three or four times, but I couldn't make it work. I went and told the widow about it, and she said the thing a body could get by praying was "spiritual gifts." She said I must do everything I could for other people and never think about myself. I went out in the woods and turned it over in my mind a long time, but I couldn't see no advantage to it, so I decided not to worry about it anymore. Sometimes the widow would take me aside and talk about Heaven in a way to make a body's mouth water. But maybe the next day Miss Watson would take hold and knock it all down again. I saw there must be two Heavens. A poor fellow would do all right in the widow's Heaven, but if Miss Watson's got him, there warn't no help for him anymore.

The gang played robbers now and then for about a month. Then I resigned. So did Ben and Joe. We hadn't robbed or killed nobody, only just pretended. We'd hop out of the woods and go charging down on hog drivers and women carting garden stuff to market, but we never robbed any of them. Tom called the hogs "gold" and the fruit and vegetables "jewelry." We'd go back to the cave and talk about how much loot we'd got, but I couldn't see no profit in it.

Chapter 2

Three or four months run along, and it was well into winter. I'd been to school almost all the time and could read and write a little and say the multiplication table up to "Six times seven is thirty-five." But I don't take no stock in mathematics.

At first I hated school, but by and by I got so I could stand it. Whenever I got uncommon tired, I played hooky. I was getting sort of used to the widow's ways, too. Living in a house and sleeping in a bed made me pretty uncomfortable, but before the cold weather I'd slip out sometimes and sleep in the woods. The widow said I was coming along slow but sure.

One morning I happened to turn over the salt shaker at breakfast. I reached for some of it as quick as I could, to throw over my left shoulder to keep off bad luck. But Miss Watson stopped me. "Take your hands away, Huckleberry!" she says. "What a mess you're always making!" The widow put in a good word for me, but that warn't going to keep off the bad luck. After breakfast I started out feeling worried and low-spirited, wondering when and where the bad luck would get me.

I went down to the front garden. There was an inch of new snow on the ground, and I see somebody's tracks. They went around the garden fence. It was odd that the person hadn't come in. I stooped down to look at the tracks and saw that the left boot-heel had a cross made with big nails, to keep off the Devil. Pap!

In a second I was running down the hill. I looked over my shoulder every now and then, but I didn't see nobody. I went to Judge Thatcher's as quick as I could.

He says, "Why, my boy, you are all out of breath. Did you come for your interest?"

"No, sir. Is there some for me?"

"Yes. A half-yearly is in last night. Over a hundred and fifty dollars, quite a fortune for you. You'd better let me invest it along with your six thousand."

"I don't want any of it," I says. "I want you to take it—six thousand and all."

Judge Thatcher looked surprised. "Why, what can you mean, my boy?"

"Please don't ask me no questions about it. Will you take it?"

"I'm puzzled. Is something the matter?"

"Please take it," I says, "and don't ask me nothing."

He thought awhile. "Oh, I think I see. You want to sell your property to me." He wrote something on a paper and read it over. "There. You see, it says 'for a consideration.' That means I have bought it from you. Here's a dollar for you. Now you sign it."

I signed it and left.

When I lit my candle and went up to my room that night, there sat Pap. At first I was scared because it was so common for him to hit me. But then I calmed down. He was almost fifty, and he looked it. His black hair was long, tangled, and greasy, including his whiskers. His eyes looked like they was behind vines. His face was a sickly white. His clothes were rags. He had one ankle resting on the other knee. The boot on that foot was busted; two of his toes stuck through. His hat was laying on the floor—an old black hat with the top caved in, like a lid.

I stood looking at him, and he set there looking at me, with his chair tilted back a little. I set the candle down. I noticed the window was up, so he had clumb in by the shed. He kept looking me over. By and by, he says, "Starchy clothes. You've put on considerable frills since I been away. I'll take you down a peg before I'm done with you. You're educated, they say—can read and write. You think you're better than me now, don't you? You drop that school, you hear? I won't have you putting on airs over your own father. Let me hear you read."

I took up a book and begun something about George Washington. When I'd read about half a minute, Pap knocked the book across the room. He says, "It's true, then. I had my doubts. If I catch you around that school, I'll tan you good. First thing you know, you'll get religion, too." He took up a little picture of some cows and a boy. "What's this?"

"Something they give me for learning my lessons good."

He tore it up. "So here you are with a bed and bedclothes, and a mirror, and a piece of carpet on the floor, and your own father's got to sleep with the hogs in the tannery. They say you're rich."

"I'm not."

"Don't you lie to me. I've been in town two days, and I ain't heard nothing but about you bein' rich. I heard about it away down the river, too. That's why I come. You git me that money tomorrow. I want it."

"I ain't got no money. You ask Judge Thatcher. He'll tell you the same."

"All right, I'll ask him. I'll make him pay out, too. How much you got in your pocket?"

"Only a dollar, and I want that to . . ."

"Hand it over." He took it and said he was going downtown to get some whisky. He left.

The next day, Pap was drunk. He went to Judge Thatcher and tried to make him give up the money, but he couldn't. Then Pap swore he'd make the law force Judge Thatcher.

Judge Thatcher and the widow tried to get the court to take me away from Pap and let one of them be my guardian. But the judge that heard the case was a newcomer who didn't know Pap. He said courts mustn't separate families if they could help it. He said he'd rather not take a child away from his father. So Judge Thatcher and the widow had to quit on the business.

That pleased Pap no end. He said he'd beat me 'til I was black and blue if I didn't give him some money. I borrowed three dollars from Judge Thatcher. Pap took it and got drunk. He went around cussing, whooping, and carrying on. He kept it up all over town, with a tin pan, 'til almost midnight. Then they jailed him. The next day, they had him before the court and jailed him again, for a week.

When Pap got out, the new judge said he was going to make a man of him. He took Pap to his own house, dressed him up clean and nice, and had him to breakfast, lunch, and supper with his family. After supper he talked to Pap about avoiding liquor and such things. Pap cried and said he'd fooled away his life. He said he was going to turn over a new leaf and be a man nobody would be ashamed of. He said he hoped the judge would help him and not look down on him. The judge said he could hug Pap for them words.

When it was bedtime, Pap got up, held out his hand, and says, "Look at it, ladies and gentlemen. That was the hand of a hog. Now it's the hand of a man that's starting a new life and that'll die before he'll go back to his old ways. It's a clean hand now. Shake it." And they all did. Pap made a pledge, and the judge said it was a holy time. They gave Pap a beautiful room to sleep in.

Some time during the night, Pap got powerful thirsty, sneaked out, and got drunk. When he tried to climb back into his room, he fell and broke his left arm in two places. When somebody found him after sunup, he was almost froze to death. The judge felt kind of sore. He said he reckoned a body could reform Pap with a shotgun, maybe, but no other way.

Chapter 3

Pretty soon Pap was up and around again. He went for Judge Thatcher in the courts to make him give up the money. And he went for me for not stopping school. He catched me a couple of times and thrashed me, but I went to school just the same and dodged him or outrun him most of the time. I didn't want to go to school much before, but I reckoned I'd go now to spite Pap.

The law trial was slow business. It appeared they warn't ever going to get started on it. So every now and then I borrowed two or three dollars off of Judge Thatcher for Pap, to keep from getting hit. Every time Pap got money, he got drunk. And every time he got drunk, he raised a ruckus around town. And every time he raised a ruckus, he got jailed.

Pap got to hanging around the widow's too much. She told him that if he didn't quit it, she'd make trouble for him. He was hopping mad. He said he'd show who was Huck Finn's boss.

One day in the spring, Pap watched for me and catched me. He took me up the river about three mile in a skiff and crossed over to the Illinois shore where there warn't no houses, only an old log cabin in thick woods.

Pap and me lived in that cabin, and I never got a chance to run off. He always locked the door and put the key under his head at night. He had a gun that he must've stole; we hunted and fished, and that was what we lived on. Every little while, he locked me in and went down, three miles, to the store and traded fish and game for whisky. He fetched the whisky home and got drunk and beat me.

By and by, the widow found out where I was and sent a man over to try to get hold of me. Pap drove him off with the gun.

Soon I was used to being where I was, and liked it—all but the beatings. It was kind of lazy and jolly to lay around comfortable all day, smoking and fishing, and no books or study. Two months or more run along, and my clothes got to be all rags and dirt. I didn't see how I'd ever got to like it at the widow's, where you have to wash, eat on a plate, comb your hair, go to bed regular, get up regular, always be bothering over a book, and have Miss Watson pecking at you all the time. I didn't want to go back no more. I had stopped cussing because the widow didn't like it, but now I took to it again because Pap hadn't no objections.

All around, it was pretty good times up there in the woods.

But by and by, Pap got too handy with his hickory switch. I was all over welts. He got to going away a lot, too, and locking me in. Once he locked me in and was gone three days. It was dreadful lonesome. I judged he had drownded, and I wasn't ever going to get out. I was scared. I made up my mind I would figure out some way to leave. I had tried to get out of that cabin many a time, but I couldn't find no way. There warn't a window big enough for a dog to get through. I couldn't get up the chimney; it was too narrow. The door was thick oak slabs. Pap was careful not to leave a knife or anything in the cabin when he was away. I reckon I'd searched the place a hundred times.

I found something at last: a rusty old saw without a handle. I greased it up and went to work. At the cabin's far end there was an old blanket nailed against the logs behind the table, to keep the wind from blowing through the chinks and putting the candle out. I got under the table, raised the blanket, and went to work sawing out a big section of the bottom log—big enough to let me through. It was a good, long job. I was getting towards the end of it when I heard Pap's gun in the woods. I got rid of the signs of my work, dropped the blanket, and hid the saw.

Pretty soon Pap come in. He warn't in a good

mood, just his natural self. He said he was down-town and everything was going wrong. His lawyer said he reckoned Pap would win his lawsuit and get the money if they ever got started on the trial, but there was ways to put it off a long time, and Judge Thatcher knowed how to do it. Pap said people figured there'd be another trial to get me away from him and give me to the widow for my guardian, and they guessed the widow would win. This shook me up because I didn't want to go back to the widow's anymore and be so cramped up and civilized. Pap cussed everybody he could think of, cussed them all again to make sure he hadn't skipped anybody, and finished with a cuss that included a considerable parcel of people he called "What's-his-name" because he didn't know their names. He said he'd like to just see the widow get me. He said if they tried to pull any such game on him, he'd put me in a place seven mile off where they might hunt 'til they dropped and never find me.

I reckoned I wouldn't stay around 'til he got that chance.

Pap made me go to the skiff and fetch the things he'd got. There was a fifty-pound sack of cornmeal, a side of bacon, ammunition, and a four-gallon jug of whiskey. I toted a load, went back, and set down on the skiff to rest. I thought it all over and reckoned I'd take the gun and some fishing lines and run away to the woods. I'd tramp right across the country, mostly nights, and hunt and fish to keep alive. I'd get so far away that Pap and the widow couldn't ever find me. I'd saw my way out and leave that night if Pap got drunk enough. I got so full of thinkin' that I didn't notice how long I was staying 'til Pap hollered and asked me whether I was asleep or drownded.

By the time I got all the things up to the cabin, it was about dark. While I was cooking supper, Pap took some swigs of whiskey and went to ripping again. He'd been drunk over in town and laid in the gutter all night. He was a sight to look at—all mud.

Whenever his liquor begun to work, Pap almost always went for the government. This time he says, "Call this a gov'ment? Just look at it! Here's the law ready to take a man's son away from him—a man's own son, which he has had all the trouble and expense of raising. Just as that son is ready to go to work and begin to do somethin' for his father, the law up and tries to take him away. The law backs that old Judge Thatcher and helps him keep me out o' my property. Oh, yes, this is a wonderful gov'ment! There was a free nigger in town, from Ohio—a mulatto, almost as white as a white man. He had the whitest shirt you ever saw, and the shiniest hat. There ain't a man in that town that's got as fine clothes as what he had. That nigger had a gold watch and chain and a silver-headed cane. And what do you think? They said he was a pr'fessor in a college and could talk all kinds of languages and knowed everything. And that ain't the worst. They said he could *vote* when he was at home. What's this country comin' to? It was election day, and I was about to go and vote if I warn't too drunk to get there, but when they told me there was a state in this country where they'd let a nigger vote, I says, 'I'll never vote again as long as I live.' And to see the cool way of that nigger! Why, he wouldn't 've give me the road if I hadn't shoved him out o' the way. I says to people, 'Why ain't this nigger put up at auction and sold?' And what do you reckon they said? They said he couldn't be sold 'til he'd been in the state six months, and he hadn't been there that long. You call that a gov'ment? A gov'ment that won't let you sell a prowlin', thievin', infernal, white-shirted nigger?"

After supper Pap started drinking again. I judged he'd be blind drunk in about an hour. Then I'd steal the key or saw my way out. He tumbled down onto his blankets, but luck didn't run my way. He didn't fall sound asleep but was uneasy. He groaned and moaned and thrashed around for a long time. At last I got so sleepy that I couldn't keep my eyes open. Before I knowed it, I was sound asleep.

Chapter 4

The next morning, Pap woke me saying, "Out with you. See if there's a fish on the lines for breakfast. I'll be along in a minute."

He unlocked the door, and I cleared out up the riverbank. I noticed some tree limbs floating down, so I knowed the river had begun to rise. I reckoned I'd have great times now if I was over at the town because as soon as the river starts to rise, cordwood and pieces of log rafts come floating down—sometimes a dozen logs together. All you have to do is catch them and sell them to wood yards and the sawmill.

I went up the bank with one eye lookin' out for Pap and the other lookin' out for what the river might bring along. All at once here comes a drift canoe—a beauty about thirteen foot long—riding high, like a duck. Clothes and all on, I leaped headfirst off of the bank and struck out for the canoe. I clumb in and paddled her ashore. I thought, "Pap will be glad when he sees this. She's worth ten dollars."

But when I got to shore, Pap warn't in sight. As I run the canoe into a little creek, all hung over with vines and willows, I struck another idea: I'd hide her good; instead of taking to the woods when I run off, I'd go down the river about fifty mile and camp in one place for good. That would be less rough than tramping on foot.

I was pretty close to the cabin, and I thought I heard Pap coming. But I got the canoe hid. Then I looked around a bunch of willows. There was Pap down the path a piece, aiming his gun at a bird. So he hadn't seen me. When he come along, I was taking up a fishing line. He abused me a little for being so slow, and I told him I fell in the river. (I knowed he'd see I was wet.) We got five catfish off the lines and went home.

After breakfast I got to thinking that if I could figure out some way to keep Pap and the widow from trying to follow me, it would be a certainer thing than trusting to luck to get far enough off before they missed me. Then I figured out a way.

About noon Pap and me went along up the bank. The river was coming up pretty fast, and lots of driftwood was going by. By and by, along comes part of a log raft—nine logs fast together. We went out with the skiff and towed it ashore. Then we had lunch. Anybody but Pap would've waited to catch more stuff, but that warn't his style. Nine logs was enough for him. He wanted to shove right over to town and sell.

About half past three he locked me in. He took the skiff and started off, towing the raft. I judged he wouldn't come back that night. I waited 'til I reckoned he'd got a good start. Then I went out with my saw and went to work on that log again. Before Pap was on the other side of the river, I was out of the hole. Him and his raft was just a speck on the water away off yonder.

I took the sack of cornmeal to where the canoe was hid. I shoved the vines and branches apart and put the cornmeal into the canoe. Then I done the same with the side of bacon and the whiskey jug. I took all the coffee and sugar there was and all the ammunition. I took a dipper, a tin cup, the old saw, two blankets, the frying pan, the coffee pot, fishing lines, matches—everything that was worth a cent. I cleaned the place out. I fetched out the gun and was done.

I had wore the ground a good deal crawling out of the hole and dragging out so many things, so I fixed that as good as I could from the outside by scattering dirt on the place. The dirt covered up the smoothness and the sawdust. Then I put the piece of log back in its place and put two rocks under it and one against it, to hold it there, because it was bent up at that place and didn't quite touch the ground. If you stood a few foot away and didn't know it was sawed, you wouldn't never notice it. Besides, this was the back of the cabin; it warn't likely anybody would go fooling around there. It was all grass, clear to the canoe, so I hadn't left a track.

I stood on the bank and looked out over the river. All safe. I took the gun and went up a piece into the woods. I was hunting around for a bird when I see a wild pig. I shot the pig and took his body to the cabin.

I took an ax and smashed in the door. I hacked it considerable. I fetched the pig in, took him back nearly to the table, hacked into his throat with the ax, and laid him down on the ground to bleed. (I say ground because it *was* ground, hard-packed and no boards.) Next I took an old sack and put a lot of rocks in it—all I could drag. I started the dragging where the pig was and dragged the sack to the door and through the woods down to the river. I dumped the sack in, and down it sunk, out of sight. You could see, easy, that something had been dragged over the ground. I wished Tom Sawyer was there. I knowed he'd take an interest in this kind of business and throw in fancy touches.

I put lots of pig's blood on the ax, pulled out some of my hair and stuck it on the ax, and slung the ax in a corner. Then I wrapped the pig in my jacket, so he wouldn't drip. I held him to my chest 'til I got a good piece below the house and then dumped him into the river. Now I thought of something else. I went and got the sack of corn-meal and old saw out of the canoe and fetched them to the house. I took the sack to where it used to stand and ripped a hole in the bottom of it with the saw. (There warn't no knifes or forks on the place. Pap used his pocketknife for cooking and eating.) I carried the sack about a hundred yards across the grass and through the willows east of the house, to a shallow lake that was five mile wide and full of bulrushes. There was a creek leading out of it on the other side that went miles away. The cornmeal sifted out and made a little track all the way to the lake. Then I tied up the rip in the cornmeal sack with a string, so it wouldn't leak no more, and took the sack and the saw back to the canoe.

It was about dark now. I took the canoe down the river, to under some willows that hung over the bank. I fastened the canoe to a willow and waited for the moon to rise. Then I took a bite to eat.

By and by, I laid down in the canoe to smoke a pipe and lay out a plan. I says to myself, "They'll follow the track of that sackful of rocks to the shore and then drag the river for me. They'll follow the cornmeal track to the lake and go browsing down the creek that leads out of it to find the robbers that killed me and took the things. They won't ever search the river for anything but my dead carcass. They'll soon get tired of that and won't bother no more about me. I can stop anywhere I want to. Jackson's Island is good enough for me. I know that island pretty well, and nobody ever comes there. I can paddle over to town nights, slink around, and pick up things I want. Jackson's Island is the place."

I was pretty tired, and the first thing I knowed I was asleep. When I woke up, I didn't know where I was for a minute. I set up and looked around, a little scared. Then I remembered. The river looked miles and miles across. The moon was so bright I could've counted the drift logs that went slipping along, black and still, hundreds of yards out from shore. Everything was dead quiet. It looked late and smelled late. You know what I mean. I don't know the words to put it in.

I took a good stretch and was just going to unhitch and start when I heard a sound away over the water. Pretty soon I made it out. It was that dull, regular sound that comes from oars working in rowlocks when it's a still night. I peeped out through the willow branches and saw a skiff away across the water. It kept coming. When it was abreast of me, I see there was one man in it. He dropped below me with the current. By and by, he came swinging up shore in the easy water. He went by so close that I could've reached out the gun and touched him. It was Pap!

I didn't lose no time. The next minute I was spinning downstream soft but quick in the shade of the bank. I went two and a half miles. Then I struck out about a quarter of a mile towards the middle of the river. (Pretty soon I'd be passing the ferry landing; I didn't want nobody to see me and hail me.) I got out amongst the driftwood, laid down in the bottom of the canoe, and let her float.

I had a good rest and a smoke, looking away into the sky, not a cloud in it. The sky looks ever so deep when you lay down on your back in the moonlight. And how far a body can hear on the water such nights!

I was away below the ferry now. I got up, and there was Jackson's Island about two and a half miles downstream, heavy timbered and standing up out of the middle of the river, big and dark and solid. There warn't any signs of the sandbar at the head of the island. It was all underwater now.

It didn't take me long to get to the island. The current was so swift that I shot past the head at a ripping rate. Then I got into the calm water and landed on the side towards the Illinois shore. I run the canoe into a deep dent in the bank that I knowed about. I had to part the willow branches to get in. When I tied it up, nobody could've seen the canoe from the outside.

I went up and set down on a log at the head of the island. I looked out on the big river and the black driftwood and away over to the town, three mile away, where there was three lights twinkling. There was a little gray in the sky now, so I stepped into the woods and laid down for a nap before breakfast.

Chapter 5

When I waked, the sun was up so high that I judged it was after eight o'clock. I laid in the grass and the cool shade, thinking about things and feeling rested and ruther satisfied. I could see the sun through a hole in the treetops, but mostly it was big trees all around and gloomy in there amongst them. There was freckled places on the ground where the light sifted down through the leaves. The freckled places swapped around a little, showing there was a little breeze up there. A couple of squirrels set on a limb and jabbered at me very friendly.

I was powerful lazy and comfortable. I didn't want to get up and cook breakfast. I was dozing off again when I hear a deep boom away up the river. I rouses up onto my elbow and listens. Pretty soon I hears it again. I hopped up and went and looked out through a hole in the leaves. I see a bunch of smoke laying on the water a long ways up, about abreast of the ferry. And there was the ferryboat, full of people floating along down. I knowed what was the matter now. Boom! I see the white smoke squirt out of the ferryboat's side. They was a cannon firing over the water, trying to make my carcass come to the top.

I was pretty hungry, but it wouldn't do for me to start a fire because they might see the smoke. So I set there and watched the cannon smoke and listened to the booms. The river was a mile wide there, and it always looks pretty on a summer morning, so I was having a good enough time seeing them hunt for my remainders if I only had a bite to eat. Then I happened to think how they always put mercury in loaves of bread and float them off because they go right to the drownded carcass and stop there. So I figured I'd keep a lookout for any loaves that might go floating by. I changed to the island's Illinois edge, where the current set in closest to the shore. Sure enough, a big double loaf come along. I almost got it with a long stick, but my foot slipped, and it floated further out. By and by, another one come along, and this time I got it. I took out the plug, shook out the little dab of mercury, and set my teeth in. It was baker's bread—what rich folks eat—not rough cornbread.

I got a good place amongst the leaves and set there on a log, munching the bread and watching the ferryboat. Then something struck me: the widow or the parson or somebody must've prayed that this bread would find me, and here it had. So there ain't no doubt that there's something in praying when somebody like the widow or the parson does it. But it don't work for me. I reckon it works only when the right kind of people does it.

I lit a pipe, had a good long smoke, and went on watching. The ferryboat was floating with the current. I'd have a chance to see who was aboard when she come along because she'd come in close, where the bread did. When she got down towards me, I put out my pipe and went to where I fished out the bread. I laid down behind a log on the bank in a little open place. I could peep through where the log forked.

By and by, the ferry come along. She drifted in so close that they could've run out a plank and walked ashore. Most everybody was on the boat: Pap, Tom Sawyer, his Aunt Polly, his half-brother Sid, Judge Thatcher, and plenty more. Everybody was talking about the murder.

The captain broke in: "Look sharp now. The current sets in the closest here. Maybe he's washed ashore and got tangled in the brush at the water's edge. I hope so, anyway."

I didn't hope so. They all crowded up and leaned over the rails, nearly in my face, and kept still, watching with all their might. I could see them first-rate, but they couldn't see *me*.

Then the captain called out, "Stand away!" The cannon let off such a blast right before me that it made me deaf with the noise and near blind with the smoke. If they'd had some bullets in the blast, I reckon they'd 've got the corpse they was after.

The boat floated on and went out of sight around the shoulder of the island. I could hear the booming now and then, further and further off. After about an hour, I didn't hear it no more. The island was three mile long. I judged they'd got to the foot of the island and was giving up. But they didn't yet. They turned around and started up the channel on the Missouri side, under steam, booming once in a while as they went. I crossed over to that side and watched them. When they got abreast of the head of the island, they quit shooting, dropped over to the Missouri shore, and went home to the town.

I knowed I was all right now. Nobody else would come hunting after me. I got my stuff out of the canoe and made me a nice camp in the thick woods. I made a kind of tent out of blankets, to put my things under, so the rain couldn't get at them. I catched a catfish. Towards sundown I started my campfire and had supper. Then I set out a line to catch some fish for breakfast.

When it was dark, I set by my campfire, smoking and feeling pretty satisfied. But by and by it got sort of lonesome, so I went and set on the bank. I listened to the current swashing along and counted the stars and the drift logs and rafts that come down. There ain't no better way to put in time when you're lonesome. Then I went to bed.

It was pretty much the same for three days and nights. Then I explored the island. It belonged to me, so to speak. I wanted to know all about it, but mainly I wanted something to do. I found plenty of ripe strawberries, green grapes, and green razberries. Green blackberries was just beginning to show. They'd all come in handy by and by, I judged.

I went fooling along in the deep woods 'til I judged I warn't far from the foot of the island. I had my gun along for protection and maybe some hunting. About this time I almost stepped on a good-sized snake. It went sliding off through the grass and flowers. I went after it, trying to get a shot at it. All of a sudden I bounded right onto the ashes of a campfire that was still smoking!

My heart jumped into my lungs. I uncocked my gun and sneaked away as fast as I could without making too much noise. Every now and then I stopped a second amongst the thick leaves and listened, but my breath come so hard that I couldn't hear nothing else. I slunk further along and then listened again. If I saw a stump, I took it for a man. If I stepped on a stick and broke it, I felt like my breath was cut in two and I had only half—the short half.

When I got to camp, I put all my stuff into my canoe, to have it out of sight. I put out the fire and scattered the ashes around to make it look like an old campsite. Then I clumb a tree. I reckon I was up in the tree about two hours, but I didn't see or hear nothing. At last I got down, but I kept in the thick woods and on the lookout all the time. All I could eat was berries and what was left over from breakfast because I didn't dare make a campfire.

By nighttime I was pretty hungry. When it was good and dark, I slid out from shore before moonrise and paddled about a quarter of a mile to the Illinois bank. I went into the woods and cooked a supper.

I had about made up my mind that I would stay there all night when I heard the plunkety-plunk of horses coming. Next I heard people's voices. I got everything into the canoe as quick as I could. Then I went creeping through the woods to see what I could find out. I hadn't got far when I heard a man say, "We better camp here if we can find a good place. The horses is tired out. Let's look around."

I shoved out and paddled away. I tied up in the old place and reckoned I'd sleep in the canoe. But I didn't sleep much. I kept waking up, thinking that somebody had me by the neck. By and by, I says to myself, "I can't live this way. I have to find out who's here on the island with me. I'll find out or bust." I felt better right away.

I took my paddle and slid out from shore a step or two. Then I let the canoe drop down amongst the shadows. The moon was shining, and outside of the shadows it was almost as light as day. I poked along for about an hour. Everything was still as rocks and sound asleep. By this time I was down almost to the foot of the island. A little rip-ply, cool breeze begun to blow. That was as good as saying that the night was about done. I give the canoe a turn with the paddle and brung her nose to shore. Then I got my gun and slipped out and into the edge of the woods.

I set down on a log and looked out through the leaves. I see the moon go off watch and the darkness begin to blanket the river. In a little while I see a pale streak over the treetops and knowed daytime was coming.

I took my gun and slipped off towards where I'd run across that campfire, stopping every minute or two to listen. At first I couldn't find the place. Then I catched a glimpse of fire away through the trees. I went for it, cautious and slow. By and by, I was close enough to have a look.

A man laid on the ground. It almost gave me a fit of fright. He had a blanket around his head, and his head was nearly in the fire. I set there behind a clump of bushes about six foot from him and kept my eyes on him. Daylight was coming on; it was getting gray now. Pretty soon he yawned, stretched, and threw off the blanket. It was Miss Watson's Jim!

I says, "Hello, Jim!" and popped out from behind the bushes.

Jim bounced up and stared at me with a wild look. Then he drops down on his knees, puts his hands together, and says, "Don' hurt me. Don't! I ain't never done you no harm. We was frens when you was alive, an' I's still yo' fren. Please git back in de river where you belongs. Don' do nothin' to me. I always was yo' fren."

It didn't take long for me to make Jim understand that I warn't dead. I was so glad to see him! I warn't lonesome no more. I told him I warn't afraid of him telling people where I was. I talked along, but he only set there looking at me. He didn't say nothing. Then I says, "It's good daylight now. Let's get breakfast. Make up your campfire."

"What's de use o' makin' up de campfire to cook strawberries an' such? You got a gun, so we can git somethin' better dan strawberries."

"Strawberries an' such? Is that what you been livin' on?"

"I couldn' git nothin' else."

"Why, how long you been on the island, Jim?"

"I come here de night after you was killed."

"What? All that time?"

"Yes, indeedy."

"And you ain't had nothing but berries to eat?"

"No. Nothin' else."

"You must be almost starved."

"I reckon I could eat a horse. How long *you*

been on de islan'?"

"Since the night I got killed."

"What has you lived on? Oh, you got a gun, so you can hunt. Dat's good."

"I've got fishing line, too, and food I brung with me."

We went over to where the canoe was. While Jim built a fire in a grassy open place amongst the trees, I fetched cornmeal, bacon, coffee, sugar, a frying pan, a coffee pot, and tin cups. I catched a good big catfish, too. Jim cleaned it with his knife and fried it.

When breakfast was ready, Jim set to with all his might 'cause he was near starved. We ate our fill and then got to talking.

"Looky here, Huck," Jim says. "Who was it dat was killed in dat cabin if it warn't *you*?"

I told him the whole story, and he said I was smart. He said Tom Sawyer couldn't get up no better plan than I had.

Then I says, "Why are you here, Jim? How'd you get here?"

He looked uneasy and didn't say nothing for a minute. "Maybe I better not tell."

"Why, Jim?"

"Dere's reasons. You wouldn' tell on me if I was to tell you, would you, Huck?"

"Blamed if I would, Jim!"

"I believe you, Huck. I . . . run off."

"Jim!"

"Mind, you said you wouldn' tell. You said you wouldn' tell, Huck."

"I said I wouldn't, and I'll stick to it. People would call me a low-down abolitionist and despise me for keeping mum, but that don't make no difference. I ain't goin' to tell. I ain't goin' back there anyways. So tell me all about it."

"Well, it was dis way. Miss Watson—she picks on me all de time an' treats me pretty rough, but she always said she wouldn' sell me down to New Orleans. Lately I noticed a nigger trader aroun' de place and begun to git uneasy. One night I creeps to de door pretty late. It warn't quite shut. I hear Miss Watson tell de widow she goin' to sell me down to Orleans. She didn' want to, but she could git eight hundred dollars for me. It was such a stack o' money dat she couldn' resist. De widow try to git Miss Watson to say she wouldn' do it, but I didn' wait to hear de rest.

"I lit out mighty quick. I went down de hill, thinkin' I'd steal a skiff along de shore somewheres above de town. Dere still was people stirrin', so I hid in de ol' tumble-down carpenter's shop on de bank to wait for everybody to go away. Well, I was dere all night. Dere was somebody aroun' all de time.

"About six in de mornin', skiffs begun to go by. About eight or nine, every skiff dat went along was talkin' about how yo' pap come over to de town an' say you's killed. Dese last skiffs was full o' ladies an' gentlemen goin' over to see de place. Sometimes dey'd pull up at de shore an' take a rest before dey started across. From de talk, I got to know all about de killin'. I was powerful sorry you's killed, Huck.

"I laid dere under wood shavings all day. I was hungry, but I warn't afeared 'cause I knowed dat Miss Watson and de widow was goin' to a camp meeting right after breakfas' an' dat dey'd be gone all day. Dey knows dat I goes off wid de cattle about daylight, so dey wouldn' expec' to see me aroun' de place. Dey wouldn' miss me 'til after dark in de evening. De other servants wouldn' miss me 'cause dey'd take a holiday as soon as Miss Watson and de widow was out o' de way.

"When dark come, I went up de river road. I went about two mile to where dere warn't no houses. I'd made up my min' about what I was goin' to do. If I kep' on tryin' to git away on foot, de dogs would track me. If I stole a skiff to cross over, dey'd miss de skiff. Dey'd know about where I'd land on de other side an' where to pick up my track. So I thinks, 'A raft is what I's after. It don' make no track.' By an' by, I see the light of a raft comin'. I waded in. I pushed a log ahead o' me, to hide me, and swum more 'n half way across de river. I got in amongst de driftwood. I kep' my head low an' kind o' swum against de current 'til de raft come along. Den I swum to it an' took hold. It clouded up an' was pretty dark for a while, so I clumb up an' laid down on de planks. All de men was away yonder in de middle o' de raft, where de lantern was. De river was risin', an' dere was a good current, so I reckoned dat by four in de mornin' I'd be twenty-five mile down de river. I'd slip back into de water jus' befo' daylight an' swim ashore. Then I'd take to de woods on de Illinois side.

"But I didn' have no luck. When we was almost down to de head o' de islan', a man begun to come towards me wid de lantern. I see it warn't no use to wait. I slid overboard an' struck out for de islan'. I had a notion I could land almost anywheres, but I couldn't. The bank was too steep. I was almost to de foot o' de islan' befo' I found a good place.

"I went into de woods an' judged I wouldn't fool wid rafts no mo', long as dey move de lantern aroun' so much. I had tobacco, my pipe, an' some matches in my cap. Dey warn't wet, so I was all right."

"You ain't had no meat or bread all this time? Why didn't you catch mud turtles?"

"How you goin' to catch 'em? You can't slip up on 'em an' grab 'em. An' how you goin' to hit 'em wid a rock? I couldn't see well enough at night, an' I warn't goin' to show myself on de bank in de daytime."

"Well, that's so. You've had to keep in the woods all the time. Did you hear them shooting the cannon?"

"Yes. I knowed dey was after *you*. I see 'em go by here. I watched 'em through de bushes."

Some young birds come along, flying a yard or two at a time and landing. Jim said it was a sign that it was going to rain. He said it was a sign when young chickens flew that way, so he reckoned it was the same when other young birds done it. Jim knowed all kinds of signs.

Jim asked me more about why I run away. I said that bein' rich wasn't as good as I thought. It brung its own kinds of troubles.

"*I* feel rich now," Jim says, "'cause I owns *myself.*"

Chapter 6

I wanted to go look at a place, near the middle of the island, that I found when I was exploring. Jim and me soon got to it because the island was only three mile long and a quarter of a mile wide. The place was a long, steep hill about forty foot high. We had a rough time getting to the top because the sides was so steep and the bushes so thick. We tramped and clumb all over it and found a good cave in the rock, almost to the top on the side towards Illinois. The cave was as big as two or three rooms; Jim could stand up straight in it. It was cool in there.

Jim was for putting our stuff in the cave right away, but I said we didn't want to be climbing up and down all the time. Jim said if we had the canoe hid in a good place, and had all the stuff in the cave, we could rush to the cave if anybody come to the island, and they'd never find us without dogs.

So we went back, got the canoe, and paddled up abreast of the cave. We lugged all the stuff up there. Then we hunted up a place close by to hide the canoe, amongst thick willows. We took some fish off the lines, set the lines again, and begun to get ready for lunch.

The cave entrance was big enough to roll a barrel in. On one side of the entrance, the floor stuck out a little bit and was flat. It was a good place to build a fire. So we built a fire there and cooked lunch. We spread the blankets inside for a carpet and ate our lunch in there. We put all the other things at the back of the cave.

Pretty soon it darkened and begun to thunder and lighten, so Jim and the birds was right about rain coming. Directly it begun to rain like all fury. I never see the wind blow so. It was one of those regular summer storms. It got so dark that it looked all blue-black outside and lovely. The rain thrashed along so thick that the trees off a little ways looked dim and spider-webby. Here come a blast of wind that bent the trees down and turned up the pale underside of the leaves. A perfect ripper of a gust followed and set the branches to tossing their arms as if they was wild. Next, just when it was about the bluest and blackest . . . Fst! It was as bright as glory, and we had a glimpse of treetops plunging about away off yonder, hundreds of yards further than we could see before. In another second, it was dark as sin again. Now we heard the thunder let go with an awful crash and go rumbling down the sky towards the underside of the world, like empty barrels rolling downstairs.

"Jim, this is nice," I says. "I wouldn't want to be nowhere but here. Pass me another hunk of fish and some cornbread."

"Well, you wouldn' 've been here if you hadn' listened to me. You'd 've been down dere in de woods widdout any lunch an' gettin' almost drownded. Chickens knows when it's goin' to rain, an' so does other birds."

The river went on rising for more than a week, 'til it was over the banks. The water was three or four foot deep in the island's low places and over the Illinois shore. On the Illinois side the river was a good many miles wide. But on the Missouri side it was the same old distance across—half a mile—because the Missouri shore was a high wall of bluffs.

Daytimes we paddled all over the island in the canoe. It was mighty cool and shady in the deep woods, even if the sun was blazing outside. We went winding in and out amongst the trees. Sometimes the vines hung so thick that we had to back away and go some other way. On every broken-down tree you could see rabbits and snakes and such things. When the island had been over-flowed a day or two, they got so tame, on account of being hungry, that you could paddle right up and put your hand on them if you wanted to. But not the turtles and snakes; they would slide off into the water. The ridge our cave was in was full of them. We could've had plenty of pets if we'd wanted them.

One night we catched a section of a lumber raft—nice pine planks. It was twelve foot wide and about fifteen foot long. The top stood above water six or seven inches—a solid, level floor. Sometimes we could see saw logs go by in the daylight, but we let them go. We didn't show ourselves in daylight.

Another night, when we was up at the head of the island just before daylight, here comes a frame house. It was a two-story and tilted over considerable. We paddled out, got aboard, and clumb in at an upstairs window. But it was too dark to see yet, so we tied the canoe fast and set in her to wait for daylight.

The light begun to come before we got to the foot of the island. Then we looked in through the window. We could make out a bed, a table, two old chairs, and lots of things on the floor. There was clothes hanging against the wall. There was something laying on the floor in the far corner that looked like a man.

Jim says, "Hello!" But it didn't budge.

So I hollered.

Then Jim says, "Dat man ain't asleep. He's dead. You hold still. I'll go see."

Jim went. He bent down and looked and says, "It's a dead man. Yes, indeedy. He's been shot in de back. I reckon he's been dead two or three days. Come in, Huck. But don' look at his face.

It's too awful."

I didn't look at the dead man at all. Jim throwed some old rags over him, but he needn't 've done it. I didn't want to see the body. There was heaps of old greasy cards scattered over the floor and old whisky bottles. All over the walls was the ignorantest kind of words and pictures made with charcoal. There was two old, dirty calico dresses, and a sunbonnet, and some women's underclothes hanging against the wall, and some men's clothes, too. We put the lot into the canoe. It might come in handy. There was a boy's old speckled straw hat on the floor. I took that, too. And there was a bottle with milk in it; it had a rag stopper for a baby to suck. We would've took the bottle, but it was broke. There was a seedy old chest and an old woven trunk with the hinges broke. The chest and trunk stood open, but there warn't nothing left in them that was of any account. The way things was scattered about, we reckoned the people left in a hurry and warn't fixed so as to carry off most of their stuff.

We got an old tin lantern; a butcher knife without a handle; a brand-new knife worth six cents in any store; a lot of candles; a tin candlestick; a tin cup; a ratty old quilt off the bed; a drawstring purse with needles, pins, buttons, and thread in it; a hatchet; some nails; a fishing line as thick as my little finger, with some monstrous hooks on it; a leather dog-collar; a horseshoe;

some bottles of medicine that didn't have no labels on them; a tolerable good comb for grooming horses; an old fiddle bow; and a wooden leg. Take it all around, we made a good haul.

When we was ready to shove off, we was a quarter of a mile below the island. It was pretty broad day, so I made Jim lay down in the canoe and cover up with the quilt because if he set up, people could tell he was a nigger from a good ways off. I paddled over to the Illinois shore and drifted down almost half a mile doing it. I crept up the calm water along the bank and didn't see nobody. We got home safe.

After breakfast I wanted to talk about the dead man and guess how he come to be killed. But Jim didn't want to. He said it would fetch bad luck, and the man's ghost might come and haunt us. He said a man that warn't buried was more likely to go haunting around than one that was planted and comfortable. That sounded reasonable, so I didn't say no more. But I couldn't keep from thinking about it and wishing I knowed who shot the man and why they done it.

Jim and me looked through the clothes we'd got and found eight dollars in silver sewed up in the lining of an old overcoat. Jim said he reckoned the people in that house stole the coat because if they'd knowed the money was there, they wouldn't 've left it. I said I reckoned they killed the man, too. But Jim didn't want to talk about that.

Chapter 7

The days went along, and the river went down between its banks again. About the first thing we done was to bait one of the big hooks with a skinned rabbit, set it, and catch a catfish that was as big as a man. She was more than six foot long and weighed over two hundred pounds. We couldn't handle her. She would've flung us into Illinois. We just set there and watched her rip and tear around 'til she drownded. She was as big a fish as ever was catched in the Mississippi, I reckon. Jim said he hadn't ever seen a bigger one. She would've been worth a good deal over at the town. They sell such fish by the pound in the market house there.

Next morning I said that things was getting slow and dull. I said I reckoned I'd slip over the river and find out what was going on. Jim liked that notion, but he said I must go in the dark and look sharp. Then he thought it over and said it would be good if I put on one of those dresses we'd found, so I'd look like a girl. That was a good idea, so we shortened one of the calico dresses, and I turned up my trouser legs to my knees and got into it. Jim fastened it behind with the hooks, and it was a fair fit. I put on the sunbonnet and tied it under my chin. The rim stuck out far and kept my face in shadow. Jim said nobody would know me, even in the daytime. I practiced all day to get the hang of wearing a dress. Jim said I didn't walk like a girl and I must stop pulling up the dress to reach into my pants pocket. I took notice and done better.

Just after dark I started up the Illinois shore in the canoe. I started across to the town from a little below the ferry landing. The drift of the current fetched me in at the bottom of the town. I tied up and started along the bank.

There was a light burning in a little cabin that hadn't been lived in for a long time. I wondered who had took up quarters there. I sneaked up and peeped in at the window. A woman about forty years old was knitting by a candle that was on a pine table. I figured she must be new in the town because I didn't know her face. This was lucky because I was starting to feel afraid that I had come. People might know my voice and find me out. But if this woman had been in such a little town a short time, she could tell me all I wanted to know without finding me out. So I knocked at the door and made up my mind I wouldn't forget to act like a girl.

"Come in," the woman says. And I did. She

says, "Take a chair." I done that, too. She looked me all over and says, "What's your name?"

"Sarah Williams."

"Where do you live? In this neighborhood?"

"No, ma'am. In Hookerville, seven mile below. I've walked all the way, and I'm all tired out."

"Hungry, too, I reckon. I'll find you something to eat."

"No, ma'am. I ain't hungry. I was so hungry that I stopped two mile below here at a farm. So I ain't hungry no more. It's what makes me so late. My mother's sick and out of money, and I come to tell my uncle Abner Moore. My mother says he lives at the town's upper end. I ain't ever been here before. Do you know him?"

"No, but I don't know everybody yet. I've lived here only two weeks. It's a considerable ways to the town's upper end. You better stay here tonight. Take off your bonnet."

"No. I'll rest awhile and go on. I ain't afeared of the dark."

She said she wouldn't let me go by myself. Her husband would be in by and by, maybe in an hour and a half, and she'd send him along with me.

Then she got to talking about her husband, her relatives up the river, her relatives down the river, how much better off she and her husband used to be, and how they didn't know if they'd made a mistake coming to St. Petersburg. She talked on and on, 'til I feared I'd made a mistake coming to her to find out what was going on in the town. But by and by she got around to Pap and the murder. Now I was happy to let her chatter along. She told about Tom Sawyer and me finding the six thousand dollars (only she said it was ten thousand). And she told about Pap and how bad he was. At last she got down to where I was murdered.

I says, "Who done it? We've heard considerable about this down in Hookerville, but we don't know who killed Huck Finn."

"Well, lots of people here would like to know who killed him. Some think old Finn done it."

"Is that so?"

"Almost everybody thought so at first. Old Finn never will know how close he come to getting lynched. But before night they changed their minds and judged it was done by a runaway nigger named Jim."

"Why, he . . ." I stopped. I reckoned I better keep still.

She run on and never noticed I'd started to talk. "The nigger run off the very night Huck Finn was killed. There's a reward out for him: three hundred dollars. There's a reward out for old Finn, too: two hundred dollars. Old Finn come to town the morning after the murder and told about it. He was out with them on the ferryboat hunt.

But right after that, he up and left. Before night they wanted to lynch him, but he was gone. Well, next day they found out the nigger was gone. They found out he hadn't been seen since ten o'clock the night the murder was done. So then they put it on *him*. Next day, old Finn come back and went boo-hooing to Judge Thatcher to get money to hunt for the nigger all over Illinois. The judge gave him some, and that evening old Finn got drunk. He was around 'til after midnight with a couple of hard-looking strangers and then went off with them. He ain't come back since, and they ain't expectin' him back 'til this thing blows over. People thinks now that old Finn killed his boy and fixed things so that folks would think robbers done it. That way he'd get Huck's money without having to bother a long time with a lawsuit. People say he was bad enough to do it. Oh, he's sly, I reckon. If he don't come back for a year, he'll be all right. You can't prove anything on him, and everything will be quieted down by then. He'll walk in and get Huck's money as easy as nothing."

"I reckon so. I don't see nothin' to stand in the way of it. Has everybody quit thinking the nigger done it?"

"Not everybody. A good many thinks he done it. They'll get the nigger pretty soon now. Maybe they can scare it out of him."

"Are they after him?"

"Well, you're innocent! Does three hundred

dollars lay around every day for people to pick up? Some folks think the nigger ain't far from here. I'm one of them. But I ain't talked it around. A few days ago I was talking with an old couple that lives next door in the log hut, and they happened to say that hardly anybody ever goes to that island over yonder that they call Jackson's Island. 'Don't anybody live there?' I says. 'No, nobody,' they says. I didn't say anymore, but I done some thinking. I was pretty certain I'd seen smoke over there, near the head of the island, a day or two before that. So I says to myself, 'Like as not that nigger's hiding over there.' Anyway, it's worth the trouble to give the place a hunt. I ain't seen any smoke since, so maybe he's gone now, if it *was* him. But my husband's going over to see—him and another man. My husband was gone up the river, but he got back today, and I told him as soon as he got here—two hours ago."

I was so uneasy I couldn't set still. I had to do something with my hands, so I took up a needle off of the table and went to threading it. My hands shook, and I was making a bad job of it. When the woman stopped talking, I looked up. She was looking at me pretty curious and smiling a little. I put down the needle and thread and says, "Three hundred dollars is a power of money. I wish my mother could get it. Is your husband going over there tonight?"

"Yes. He went uptown with the man I was

telling you about, to get a boat and see if they could borrow another gun. They'll go over after midnight."

"Couldn't they see better if they was to wait 'til daytime?"

"Yes, but the nigger could see better, too. After midnight he'll likely be asleep. They can slip around through the woods and find his campfire all the better for the dark, if he's got one."

"I didn't think of that."

The woman kept looking at me pretty curious, and I didn't feel a bit comfortable. Pretty soon she says, "What did you say your name was?"

"M . . . Mary Williams." It didn't seem to me that I said it was Mary before. Seemed to me I said it was Sarah. So I didn't look up. I felt sort of cornered and was afeared I was looking it, too.

"I thought you said it was Sarah when you first come in."

"Yes, ma'am; I did. Sarah Mary Williams. Sarah's my first name. Some calls me Sarah; some calls me Mary." I felt better then, but I wished I was out of there. I couldn't look up yet.

"Come, now. What's your real name? Bill? Tom? Bob?"

I reckon I shook like a leaf. I stood up and says, "Well, I think I'll be leavin' now."

"No, you won't. Set down and stay where you are. I ain't goin' to hurt you, and I ain't goin' to tell on you, neither. Tell me your secret. I'll keep it. What's more, I'll help you. So will my husband, if you want him to. I think you're a runaway apprentice. That's all. You've been treated bad, and you made up your mind to cut out. Bless you, child, I won't tell on you. Tell me all about it now."

So I said it wouldn't be no use to try to pretend any longer, and I would tell her everything, but she musn't go back on her promise. Then I told her my father and mother was dead. The law had bound me out to a mean old farmer in the country thirty mile back from the river. He treated me so bad that I couldn't stand it no more. He went away to be gone a couple of days, so I took my chance. I stole some of his daughter's old clothes and cleared out. I'd been three nights coming the thirty miles. I traveled nights and hid daytimes and slept. The bag of bread and meat I'd took lasted me all the way. I said I believed my uncle Abner Moore would take care of me, so I'd struck out for this town of Goshen.

"Goshen? Why, this ain't Goshen. This is St. Petersburg. Goshen's ten miles further up the river."

"Well, I got to be moving along. I'll fetch Goshen before daylight."

"Hold on a minute. I'll fix you up a snack to eat. You might want it." So she fixed a snack. "What's your real name?"

"George Peters, ma'am."

"Well, try to remember it, George. Don't forget and tell me it's Alexander before you go and then, when I catch you, say it's *George* Alexander. And don't go around women in that dress. You do a girl tolerable poor. You might fool men, but you won't fool women. I spotted you for a boy when you was threading the needle. You see, when women thread a needle, they don't hold the thread still and fetch the needle up to it; they hold the needle still and poke the thread at it. But men does it the other way, the way you done it. Now go along to your uncle, Sarah Mary Williams George Peters. If you get into trouble, send word to Mrs. Judith Loftus—which is me—and I'll do what I can to get you out of it. Keep the river road all the way. The road's rocky, and your feet'll be in a condition by the time you get to Goshen. Next time you tramp, take shoes and socks with you."

I went up the bank about fifty yards. Then I doubled back on my tracks and slipped back to where my canoe was, a good piece below the house. I jumped in and was off in a hurry. I went upstream far enough to make the head of the island and then started across. I took off the sunbonnet 'cause I didn't want no blinders on. When I was about half way across, I heard the clock begin to strike. I stops and listens. The sound come faint but clear over the water: eleven. When I struck the head of the island, I shoved right into the timber where my old camp used to be and started a good fire there on a high and dry spot.

Then I jumped into the canoe and paddled for the cave, a mile and a half below, as hard as I could. I landed and slopped through the timber, up the ridge, and into the cave. Jim was layin' sound asleep on the ground. I roused him and says, "Git up and hurry, Jim! There ain't a minute to lose. They're after us!"

Jim never asked no questions. He never said a word. But the way he worked for the next half hour showed how scared he was. By that time everything we had in the world was on our raft, and she was ready to be shoved out from the willow cove where she was hid. We put out the campfire at the cave and didn't show a candle outside after that.

I took the canoe out from the shore a piece and took a look. If there was a boat around, I couldn't see it 'cause stars and shadows ain't good to see by. We got out the raft and slipped along down in the shade, past the foot of the island. We was dead still, never saying a word.

Chapter 8

It must've been close to one o'clock when we got below the island. The raft did seem to go mighty slow. If a boat was to come along, we was going to take to the canoe and break for the Illinois shore. It was good a boat didn't come 'cause we hadn't thought to put the gun in the canoe, or a fishing line, or anything to eat. We was in too much of a sweat to think of so many things. It warn't good judgment to put everything on the raft.

If the men went to the island, I expect they found the campfire I built and watched it all night for Jim to come. Anyways, they stayed away from us, so my building the fire probably fooled them the way I wanted it to. I played it as low-down on them as I could.

When the first streak of day begun to show, we tied up to a sandbar thick with cottonwoods. The sandbar was in a big bend on the Illinois side. We hacked off cottonwood branches with the hatchet and covered the raft with them.

There was mountains on the Missouri shore and heavy timber on the Illinois side. The channel was down the Missouri shore at that place, so we warn't afraid of anybody running across us.

We laid there all day. We watched the rafts and steamboats spin down the Missouri shore and up-bound steamboats fight the big river in the middle. I told Jim all about Mrs. Loftus. Jim said she was a smart one. He said if she was to start after us, *she* wouldn't set down and watch a campfire. No, sir; she'd fetch a dog.

"Well, then, why didn't she tell her *husband* to fetch a dog?" I says.

Jim said he bet she did think of it by the time the men was ready to start. He believed they must've gone uptown to get a dog, so they lost all that time. Otherwise we wouldn't be here on a sandbar about seventeen mile below the town. No, indeedy; we'd be in St. Petersburg again.

I said I didn't care *why* they didn't get us, just so long as they didn't.

When it was beginning to get dark, we poked our heads out of the cottonwood thicket and looked up, down, and across. Nothing in sight.

Jim took up some of the raft's top planks and built a snug wigwam, to get under in blazing or rainy weather and to keep the things dry. Jim made a floor for the wigwam and raised it a foot or more above the level of the raft. Now the blankets and all the things was out of reach of steamboat waves.

In the middle of the wigwam we made a layer of dirt about six inches deep, with a frame around it to hold it in place. This was to build a fire on in sloppy or chilly weather. The wigwam would keep the fire from being seen. We made an extra steering oar, too, because one of the others might get broke on a snag or something. We fixed up a short forked stick to hang the old lantern on because we must always light the lantern whenever we see a steamboat coming downstream, to keep from getting run over.

That night, we traveled between seven and eight hours, with a current that was making over four mile an hour. We catched fish and talked, and we took a swim now and then to keep off sleepiness. It was kind of solemn, drifting down the big, still river. We laid on our backs looking up at the stars. We didn't ever feel like talking loud, and it warn't often that we laughed. When we did laugh, it was only a kind of low chuckle. We had mighty good weather that night, the next, and the next.

Every night we passed towns, some of them away up on black hillsides, nothing but a shiny bed of lights. The fifth night we passed St. Louis, and it was like the whole world lit up. In St. Petersburg they used to say there was twenty or thirty thousand people in St. Louis, but I never believed it 'til I see that wonderful spread of lights at two o'clock that still night. There warn't a sound there. Everybody was asleep.

Every night now, I slipped ashore towards ten o'clock at some little town and bought ten or fifteen cents' worth of cornmeal, bacon, or other food. Sometimes I took a chicken that warn't roosting comfortable.

Mornings, before daylight, I slipped into cornfields and borrowed a watermelon, a pumpkin, some corn, or things of that sort. Pap always said it warn't no harm to borrow things if you was meaning to pay the people back some time. But the widow said borrowing warn't anything but a soft name for stealing, and no decent body would do it. Jim said he reckoned Pap was partly right and the widow was partly right. He said we should pick out something and say we wouldn't borrow it anymore. Then, he reckoned, it wouldn't be no harm to keep borrowing the other things. So, drifting down the river, we talked it over one night, trying to make up our minds whether to drop the watermelons, corn, or what. Towards daylight we got it all settled satisfactory. We concluded to drop crabapples. We warn't feeling just right before that, but it was all comfortable now. I was glad the way it come out, too, 'cause crabapples ain't ever good.

Now and then, we shot a waterfowl that got up too early in the morning or didn't go to bed early enough in the evening. Take it all around, we lived pretty high.

Chapter 9

The fifth night below St. Louis we had a big storm after midnight, with a power of thunder and lightning. The rain poured down in a solid sheet. We stayed in the wigwam and let the raft take care of itself. When the lightning glared out, we could see a big, straight river ahead, and high, rocky bluffs on both sides.

By and by, I says, "Jim, looky yonder!" It was a steamboat that had killed herself on a rock. We was drifting straight down for her. The lightning showed her very clear. She was leaning over, with part of her upper deck above water. Well, it being late at night and stormy, and all so mysterious-like, I felt just the way any other boy would've felt when I see that wreck laying there so mournful and lonesome in the middle of the river: I wanted to get aboard her, slink around a little, and see what was there. So I says, "Let's land on her, Jim."

At first, Jim was dead against it. "I don' wan' to go foolin' aroun' on no wreck. We's doin' blame well, an' we better let blame well alone. Like as not, dere's a watchman on dat wreck."

"Watchman your grandmother!" I says. "There ain't nothin' to watch. Besides, we might borrow something worth having out of the captain's stateroom. Cigars, I bet you. They cost five cents apiece. Stick a candle in your pocket, Jim. I can't rest 'til we give her a rummaging. Do you reckon Tom Sawyer would ever go by this thing? Not for pie, he wouldn't. He'd call it an adventure. He'd land on that wreck if it was his last act."

Jim grumbled a little but give in. He said we mustn't talk any more than we could help and then talk mighty low.

The lightning showed us the wreck again just in time. We made fast where the deck was sticking up out of the water. We went sneaking down its slope, in the dark, feeling our way slow with our feet. Pretty soon we struck the forward end of the skylight and clumb onto it. The next step fetched us in front of the captain's door, which was open. Away down the hall we see a light. All in the same second we hear low voices in yonder!

Jim whispered that he was feeling powerful sick and told me to come along.

I says, "All right," and was going to start for the raft. But just then I heard a voice wail, "Please don't, boys. I swear I won't ever tell!"

Another voice said pretty loud, "It's a lie, Joe Turner. You've acted this way before. You always want more 'n your share. And you've always got it, too, because you've swore that if you didn't, you'd tell. This time you've said that one too many times."

By this time Jim was gone for the raft. I was just boiling with curiosity. I says to myself, "Tom Sawyer wouldn't back out now, so I won't either. I'm goin' to see what's goin' on here." I dropped onto my hands and knees in the little passage and crept in the dark.

Inside a stateroom I see Turner stretched on the floor, tied hand and foot. Two men were standing over him. One of them had a dim lantern in his hand. The other had a pistol; he pointed it at Turner's head and says, "I oughta blow your brains out."

Turner begged, "Please. Don't, Bill. I ain't ever gonna tell."

The man with the lantern laughed and said, "Hear him beg! If we hadn't got the best of him and tied him, he'd 've killed us both. Put up that pistol, Bill."

Bill says, "I don't want to, Jake Packard. I'm for killin' him. Didn't he kill Hatfield the same way? Don't he deserve it?"

"I don't want him killed. I've got my reasons."

Turner blubbered and said, "Bless you for them words, Jake! I'll never forget you as long as I live!"

Packard didn't take no notice of that. He hung his lantern on a nail, started towards where I was there in the dark, and motioned Bill to come.

I crawled as fast as I could about two yards, but the boat slanted, so I couldn't make very good time. To keep from getting run over and catched, I crawled into a room on the upper side.

Packard came pawing along in the dark. When he got to my room, he says, "Come in here."

I scrambled into the upper berth, cornered and sorry I come. Packard come in and Bill after him. They stood there, with their hands on the ledge of the berth, and talked. I couldn't see them, but I could tell where they was by the whisky on their breath. I was glad I didn't drink whisky, but it wouldn't 've made much difference 'cause I barely breathed. I was too scared. They talked low and earnest.

Bill says, "He's said he'll tell, and he will, whether or not we give him our shares. I'm for killin' him."

"So am I."

"Well, why didn't you let me do it, then?"

"There's quieter and better ways than shooting him," Packard says. "My idea is this: we'll rustle around and gather whatever pickings we've overlooked in the staterooms. Then we'll shove for shore and hide the stuff. Then we'll wait. It won't be more 'n two hours before this wreck breaks up and washes down the river. Turner will drown.

That's a considerable sight better than killin' him. It ain't good sense or good morals to kill a man when you can git around it."

"Suppose she *don't* break up?"

"Well, we can wait two hours and see, can't we?"

"All right."

So they started.

I lit out, in a cold sweat, and scrambled forward. It was dark as tar. I whispered, "Jim!"

"Huck," he answered right at my elbow, but it was a sort of moan.

"Quick, Jim! There's a gang of murderers in yonder. We've got to hunt up their boat and set her drifting down the river, so they can't get away. I want the sheriff to get them. Quick! Start the raft, and I'll . . ."

"Oh, my Lordy! Dere ain't no raft. She done broke loose an' gone. An' here we is!"

I catched my breath and almost fainted. Stuck on a wreck with murderers! We *had* to find their boat now—had to have it for ourselves.

Shaking, we worked our way down one side of the wreck, and it was slow work, too. No sign of a boat. So we prowled some more. We scrabbled forwards on the skylight, hanging on from shutter to shutter because the edge of the skylight was in the water. Then, just barely, we saw the skiff. I felt ever so thankful. In another second I would've been aboard her, but just then the door opened.

One of the men stuck his head out a couple of foot from me. I thought I was a goner, but he jerked his head back in and says, "Heave that blame lantern out o' sight, Bill!" He flung a bag of something into the boat. Then he got in himself and set down. It was Packard. Then Bill come out and got in. Packard says in a low voice, "Ready. Shove off!"

I was so weak that I couldn't hardly hang on to the shutters.

Bill says, "Hold on. Did you go through him?"

"No. Didn't you?"

"No. Then, he's still got his share o' the cash!"

"Come on, then. It ain't no use to take stuff and leave *money*."

So they got out and went in. The door slammed shut because it was on the careened side.

In half a second I was in the boat, and Jim come tumbling after me. I out with my knife and cut the rope, and away we went!

We didn't touch an oar. We didn't speak nor whisper, nor hardly even breathe. We went gliding swift along, dead silent. In a minute or two we was a hundred yards below the wreck. The darkness soaked up every last sign of her. We was safe.

When we was three or four hundred yards downstream, we see the lantern show like a little spark on the wreck, and we knowed that the rascals was beginning to understand that their boat was gone.

Jim manned the oars, and we took out after our raft.

For the first time, I begun to worry about the men. I reckon I hadn't had time to before. I begun to think how dreadful it was, even for murderers, to be in such a fix. I thought, "There ain't no telling but I might come to be a murderer myself yet, and how would *I* like drownin' on a wreck?" So I says to Jim, "As soon as we see a light, let's land a hundred yards above or below it, in a good hiding place for you and the skiff. I'll come up with some story and get somebody to go for that gang. That way, they won't drown but can be hung when their time comes."

That idea was a failure because soon it begun to storm again, worse than ever. The rain poured down. And no light showed. Everybody was in bed, I reckon. We slided down the river, watching for lights and for our raft. After a long time the rain let up, but the clouds stayed. The lightning kept up, too, but weak now.

By and by, a flash showed us a black thing floating ahead. We made for it. It was the raft! We was mighty glad to get aboard again.

We seen a light now away down to the right, on shore. I said I'd go for it. The skiff was half full of plunder that the gang had took from the wreck. We hustled it onto the raft in a pile. I told Jim to float along down, show a light when he judged he'd gone about two mile, and keep it burning 'til I come. Then I manned my oars and shoved for the light.

As I got down towards it, four more showed, up on a hillside. It was a town. I closed in above the shore light, quit rowing, and floated. As I went by, I see it was a lantern hanging on a ferryboat. I skimmed around for the watchman, wondering whereabouts he slept. By and by, I found him sleeping with his head down between his knees. I gave his shoulder two little shoves and begun to cry.

He stirred in a startled way. But when he see it was only me, he took a good yawn and stretch. "Hello, boy. What's the trouble?"

"Pap and Ma and Sis . . ." I cried some more.

"What's the matter with 'em?"

"They're . . . Are you the boat's watchman?"

"Yes. I'm the watchman, head deckhand, mate, pilot, captain, and owner, and sometimes I'm the passengers and freight."

"My pap, ma, and sis are in awful trouble. If you'd take your ferryboat and go up there . . ."

"Up where? Where are they?"

"On the wreck."

"The *Walter Scott*?"

"Yes."

"Good Lord! What are they doin' there? Why, there ain't no chance for 'em if they don't git off mighty quick!"

"About an hour after dark we come along down in our trading boat. It was so dark that we didn't notice the wreck 'til we was right on her. We hit into her, so hard that we was thrown from our boat. We grabbed onto the wreck and got aboard."

"By George! Then what did you do?"

"We hollered, but the river's so wide there that we couldn't make nobody hear. Pap said somebody got to get ashore and get help. I'm the only one that can swim, so I made a dash for it. I made land about a mile below. I asked some people for help, but they said, 'What? On a night like this, with such a current? There ain't no sense in it. You need the steam ferry.' Now, if you'll go and . . ."

"By Jackson, I'd like to, but who's goin' to pay for it? Do you reckon your pap . . ."

"My pap can't pay for it, but my uncle Jim Hornback can, easy."

"Great guns! Is *he* your uncle? Looky here; you break for that light over yonder. Turn west when you git there. About a quarter of a mile out, you'll come to a tavern. Tell them to dart you out to Jim Hornback's and he'll foot the bill. Tell him I'll have your folks all safe before he can get to town. Hurry now. I'm going up around the corner here to roust my engineer."

I struck for the light. But as soon as the ferry-man turned the corner, I went back and got into my skiff. I pulled up shore in the easy water about six hundred yards and tucked myself in amongst some boats 'cause I couldn't rest easy 'til I saw the ferryboat start.

I was feeling pretty good about myself for taking all this trouble for that gang. Not many would've done it. I wished the widow knowed about it. I judged she'd be proud of me for helping these scoundrels because scoundrels is the kind of people that the widow and other good folks takes the most interest in helping.

Before long, here comes the wreck, dim and dusky, sliding on down. A shiver went through me. I struck out for her. She'd sunk deeper now. I see in a minute there warn't much chance of anybody being alive in her. I pulled all around her and hollered a little, but there warn't no answer. It was dead still. I felt a little heavy-hearted about the gang, but not much.

Then here comes the ferryboat. I shoved for the middle of the river on a long downstream slant. When I judged I was out of eye reach, I quit rowing and looked back. I see the ferry go around the wreck awhile. Pretty soon the ferry give it up and went for shore.

I rowed fast as I could and went racing down the river. It seemed a powerful long time before Jim's light showed up. When it did, it looked like it was a thousand mile off.

By the time I got to the raft, the sky was

beginning to get a little gray in the east. Jim and me struck for an island. We hid the raft and sunk the skiff. Then we slept like dead people.

When we got up, we turned over the stuff the gang had took off of the wreck. We found boots, blankets, clothes, a spyglass, three boxes of cigars, and other things. The cigars was prime.

We laid off all the afternoon in the woods talking and having a general good time. I told Jim all about what happened inside the wreck and at the ferryboat. I said these kinds of things was adventures.

Jim said he didn't want no more adventures. He said that when I went inside the wreck and he crawled back to get on the raft and found her gone, he nearly died. He judged it was all up with him. If he didn't get saved, he'd get drownded. If he *did* get saved, whoever saved him would send him back home so as to get the reward. Then Miss Watson would sell him south for sure.

Well, he was right. He almost always was right. He had an uncommon level head for a nigger.

Chapter 10

We judged that three nights more would fetch us to Cairo, at the bottom of Illinois, where the Ohio River comes in. That was what we was after. We would sell the raft. Then we'd get on a steamboat, go way up the Ohio amongst the free states, and be out of trouble.

The second night, a fog come on. We made for a sandbar to tie the raft to because it wouldn't do to travel in fog. But when I paddled ahead in the canoe, holding the rope, there warn't anything but little saplings to tie to. I passed the line around one of them on the edge of the bank. There was a stiff current. The raft come booming down so lively that she tore the sapling out by the roots and went on past. The fog closed in, and then there warn't no raft in sight. You couldn't see twenty yards.

I jumped into the canoe, grabbed the paddle, and stroked. But the canoe didn't budge. I was in such a hurry and so scared that I hadn't untied her.

As soon as I untied her, I took out after the raft as fast as I could go, right down the sandbar. That was all right as far as it went, but the sandbar warn't sixty yards long. The minute I flew by the foot of it, I shot out into solid white fog and hadn't no more idea which way I was goin' than a dead man.

I thought, "It won't do to paddle. First thing I know, I'll run into the bank, a sandbar, or something. I've got to set still and float." It's mighty fidgety business to have to hold your hands still at such a time.

I whooped and listened. Away down somewheres I hears a small whoop. I went tearing after it, listening sharp to hear it again. The next time it come, I see I warn't heading for it but to the right of it. And the next time, I was heading to the left of it, and not gaining much either 'cause I was flying around, this way and that, but the whoop was going straight ahead all the time. I wished that Jim would beat a tin pan, and keep beating it, but he never did. The silent places between the whoops was making trouble for me. I fought along, and directly I hears the whoop behind me. I was tangled good now. Either that was somebody else's whoop, or else I was turned around.

I throwed the paddle down. I heard the whoop again—still behind me but in a different place. It kept coming and kept changing its place. I kept answering. By and by, it was in front of me again. I knowed then that the current had swung the canoe's head downstream. I was all right if that was Jim hollering and not some other raftsman. I couldn't tell one voice from another 'cause nothing sounds natural in a fog.

The whooping went on. In about a minute I come racing down on a bank with smoky ghosts of big trees on it. The current throwed me off to the left and shot by, roaring through a lot of snags. In another second it was solid white and still again. I set perfectly still, listening to my heart thump.

Then I knowed what the matter was. That bank was an island. Jim had gone down the other side of it. It warn't no sandbar that you could float by in ten minutes. It had the big timber of a regular island. It might be five or six mile long and more than half a mile wide.

I kept quiet, with my ears cocked, about fifteen minutes. I was floating along, four or five miles an hour. But you don't think of that. You feel like you're setting dead still on the water. If a glimpse of a snag slips by, you don't think to yourself how fast you're going. You just catch your breath and think, "My, how that snag's tearing along!" It's mighty lonesome and dismal out by yourself in a fog in the night.

For about half an hour, I whoops now and then. At last I hears the answer a long ways off. I tried to follow it, but I couldn't. I soon judged I'd got into a nest of sandbars. I had dim glimpses of them on both sides of me. Sometimes there was just a narrow channel between them. Some of them I couldn't see at all, but I knowed they was there because I'd hear the current wash against the dead brush that hung over the banks. Before long, I lost the whoops amongst the sandbars. You never knowed a sound to swap places so quick. A few times I had to claw away from the bank pretty lively. I judged the raft must be bumping into the bank now and then. Otherwise it would get further ahead and clear out of hearing. It seemed to be floating a little faster than I was.

By and by, I seemed to be in the open river again. I couldn't hear no whoop nowheres. I reckoned Jim had fetched up on a snag. Maybe he was drownded.

I was good and tired, so I laid down in the canoe and said I wouldn't bother no more. I didn't want to sleep, but I was so sleepy that I couldn't help it.

When I waked up, the stars was shining bright, the fog was all gone, and I was spinning down a big bend. At first I didn't know where I was. I thought I was dreaming. Then things begun to come back to me. It was a monstrous big river here, with a wall of tall, thick timber on each bank.

I looked away downstream and seen a black speck on the water. I took after it. But when I got to it, it warn't nothing but a couple of logs tied together. Then I seen another speck and chased *that*. Then another. This time I was right. It was the raft.

When I got to it, Jim was setting there, asleep, with his head down between his knees. His right arm was hanging over the steering oar. The other oar was smashed off, and the raft was littered with branches, leaves, and dirt. So he'd had a rough time.

I tied the canoe to the raft, boarded the raft, and laid down under Jim's nose. Then I began to yawn and stretch. "Hello, Jim," I says. "Have I been asleep? Why didn't you wake me?"

"Goodness gracious, is dat you, Huck? You ain't drownded! It's too good for true. Lemme look at you, chil'. De same ol' Huck, thanks to goodness!"

"What's the matter with you, Jim? What makes you talk so wild?"

"How does I talk wild?"

"Why, ain't you been talking as if I'd been away?"

"Huck Finn, you look me in de eye. Ain't you been away?"

"I ain't been nowheres, Jim. Where would I go?"

"Didn't you tote out de line in de canoe, to make fast to de sandbar?"

"No. What sandbar?"

"Looky here. Didn't de line pull loose an' de raft go shootin' down de river, leavin' you and de canoe behin' in de fog?"

"What fog?"

"De fog dat's been aroun' all night! An' didn' you whoop, an' didn' *I* whoop, 'til we got mixed up in de islands? An' didn' I bust up against a lot o' dem islands an' have a terrible time an' almost git drownded?"

"I ain't seen no fog, nor islands, nor troubles, nor nothing. I been setting here talking with you all night 'til you went to sleep about ten minutes ago, and I reckon I done the same. You've been dreaming."

"Dad fetch it, how is I goin' to dream all dat in ten minutes? An' if I dreamed it, how come I's so worn out?"

"Well, you *did* dream it because there didn't any of it happen."

Jim didn't say nothing for about five minutes but set there thinking it over. Then he says, "Well, den I reckon I did dream it, but it sure seemed real."

"Tell me about it, Jim."

So Jim went to work and told me the whole thing right through, just as it happened. Only he painted it up a bit.

It had clouded up pretty dark just after I got on the raft. But it was clearing again now. I says, "Well, that's some dream, Jim. But if you dreamed everything, what's all *this*?" I pointed to the leaves and rubbish on the raft and the smashed oar. You could see them first-rate now.

Jim looked at the trash, then at me, then back at the trash. After a while, he looked at me steady without a hint of a smile. "What's all *dis*? I'll tell you what all *dis* is. When I got all wore out wid work an' wid callin' for you, an' went to sleep, my heart was almost broke 'cause I thought you was lost. I didn' care no mo' what become o' me an' de raft. When I wake up an' find you back all safe an' soun', de tears come—I was so thankful. But all you was thinkin' was how you could make a fool of me wid a lie. So, what's all dis rubbish lyin' here on the raft? It's trash. An' *dat's* what people is dat puts dirt on de head of deir frens and makes 'em feel ashamed." Then he got up slow. He walked to the wigwam and went in without saying another word.

I felt so mean and low-down, I almost could've kissed his foot to take back what I done. It was fifteen minutes before I could work myself up to go and humble myself to a nigger. But that's what I done. And I warn't ever sorry for it afterwards, neither. I didn't do Jim no more mean tricks, and I wouldn't 've done *that* one if I'd knowed it would make him feel that way.

Chapter 11

We slept almost all day and started out at night. We went drifting down into a big bend, and the night clouded up and got hot. The river was very wide and was walled with solid timber on both sides. You couldn't hardly see a break in the timber, or a light.

Jim and me talked about Cairo. We wondered whether we'd know it when we got to it. I said likely we wouldn't because I'd heard there warn't but a dozen houses there. If they didn't happen to have them lit up, how was we going to know we was passing a town?

Jim said if two big rivers joined there, that would show.

But I said we might think we was passing the foot of an island and coming into the same old river again.

That disturbed Jim—and me. We didn't know what to do.

I said I could paddle ashore the first time a light showed and tell people that my father was behind, coming along with a trading boat. I could say that he was new at the business and wanted to know how far it was to Cairo.

Jim thought this was a good idea, so we took a smoke on it and waited. There warn't nothing to do now but look out sharp for the town and not pass it without seeing it.

Jim said he *had* to see it because if he did, he'd be a free man, but if he missed it, he'd be stuck in slave country. Every little while he jumped up and said, "Is dat Cairo?" But it warn't. It was lanterns or fireflies. So he set down and went to watching, same as before. Jim said it made him all trembly and feverish to be so close to freedom.

It made *me* all trembly and feverish, too— because I begun to get it through my head that Jim was almost free. And who was to blame for it? Me! I couldn't get that out of my conscience. It got to troubling me so that I couldn't rest. I tried to make out to myself that I warn't to blame because *I* didn't run Jim off from his rightful owner. But it warn't no use. Every time, my conscience up and says, "But you knowed he was running for his freedom. You could've paddled ashore and told somebody. What has poor Miss Watson ever done that you could see her nigger go off right under your eyes and never say a word? She tried to learn you reading. She tried to learn you manners. She tried to be good to you every way she knowed how. *That's* what she done."

I got to feeling so mean that I almost wished I was dead. I fidgeted up and down the raft while Jim fidgeted up and down past me. Every time he danced around and says, "Dere's Cairo!" it went through me like a shot. I thought if it *was* Cairo, I'd die of miserableness.

Jim said that the first thing he'd do when he got to a free state would be to save money and never spend a single cent. When he had enough, he'd buy his wife. She was owned on a farm close to where Miss Watson lived. Then him and his wife would work to buy their two children. If their master wouldn't sell them, Jim and his wife would get an abolitionist to go and steal them.

It froze me to hear such talk. Before, Jim wouldn't ever've dared to talk such talk. Just see what a difference it made in him the minute he judged he was almost free! It was according to the old saying: "Give a nigger an inch, and he'll take a mile." I thought, "This is what comes of my not thinking." Here was this nigger, which I'd as good as helped to run away, saying right out that he would steal his children—children that belonged to a man I didn't even know, a man that hadn't ever done me no harm. I was sorry to hear Jim say that he would steal his children; that was such a lowering of him. My conscience heated up so much that at last I says to it, "Let up on me. It ain't too late. I'll paddle ashore at first light and tell." I felt better right off. I went to looking out sharp for a light. By and by, one showed.

Jim sings out, "We's safe, Huck. We's safe! Jump up and crack yo' heels! Dat's good ol' Cairo at last!"

"I'll take the canoe and go and see, Jim. It might *not* be."

Jim jumped and got the canoe ready. He put his old coat in the bottom for me to set on and give me the paddle. As I shoved off, he says, "Pretty soon I'll be shoutin' for joy. An' I'll say, 'It's all on account o' Huck. I's a free man, an' I couldn' ever've been free if it hadn' been for Huck.' I won't ever forget you, Huck. You's de bes' fren I's ever had. An' you's de *only* fren I's got now. You's de only white man dat ever kep' a promise to me."

I was paddling off, all in a sweat to tell on him. But when he said this, I felt sick. I went along slow then. I told myself, "I've *got* to do it. I've *got* to do it." Right then along comes a skiff with two men in it with guns. They stopped, and I stopped.

One of them says, "What's that yonder?"

"A raft," I says.

"Do you belong on it?"

"Yes, sir."

"Any men on it?"

"Only one, sir."

"There's five niggers run off tonight, above the bend. Is your man white or black?"

I tried for a second or two to brace up and out

with it, but I warn't man enough. I give up trying and says, "He's white."

"I reckon we'll go and see for ourselves."

"I wish you would because my pa is there. Maybe you'd help me tow the raft ashore. He's sick."

"We're in a hurry, boy. But I suppose we've got to. Paddle along with us. Let's go."

When we'd made a stroke or two, I says, "Pap'll be much obliged to you. Everybody goes away when I want them to help tow the raft ashore, and I can't do it by myself."

"Well, that's odd. What's the matter with your father?"

"It's the . . . Well, it ain't anything much."

They stopped pulling. It warn't but a little ways to the raft now. One says, "Boy, I believe you're lying. What *is* the matter with your pa? Answer up square."

"I will, sir. But don't leave us. Please. It's the . . . the . . . If you'll only pull ahead and let me heave you the line, you won't have to come near the raft. Please do that."

"Set her back, John! Set her back!" one says. They backed up. "Keep away, boy. Confound it, your pa's got smallpox, don't he? Why didn't you come out and say so? Do you want to spread it all over?"

I started crying. "Well, I've told everybody before, and they just went away."

"We're right sorry for you, but we . . . Well, hang it, we don't want smallpox. Look here, I'll tell you what to do. Don't try to land by yourself. You'll smash everything to pieces. Float along down about twenty miles, and you'll come to a town on the left-hand side of the river. It will be long after sunup then. When you ask for help, say that your pa is down with chills and fever. It wouldn't do any good to land yonder where the light is. It's only a wood yard. I reckon your father's poor. He's in pretty hard luck. Here. I'll put a twenty-dollar gold piece on this board. You get it when it floats by. I feel mighty mean to leave you, but it won't do to fool with smallpox."

"Hold on, Parker," the other man says. "Here's a twenty to put on the board for *me*. Good-bye, boy. Do as Mr. Parker told you, and you'll be all right."

"Good-bye. If you see any runaway niggers, get help and nab them. You can make some money by it."

"Good-bye," I says, "I won't let no runaway niggers get by me if I can help it."

They went off, and I got aboard the raft. I felt bad and low because I knowed I'd done wrong. I see it warn't no use for me to try to do right. A body that don't get started right when he's little ain't got a chance. When the pinch comes, there ain't no experience at doin' right to back him up. Then I thought, "Hold on. Suppose I'd done right and give Jim up. Would I feel better than I do now? No," I thinks. "I'd feel bad—same as I do now. Well, then," I thinks, "what's the use of learning to do right when it's troublesome to do right and ain't no trouble to do wrong, and the wages is the same?" I couldn't answer that. So I reckoned I wouldn't bother no more about it. After this, I'd just always do whichever come handiest at the time.

I went into the wigwam. Jim warn't there. I looked all around. Jim warn't anywhere. I says, "Jim!"

"Here I is, Huck. Is dey out o' sight? Don' talk loud." He was in the river with just his nose out. I told him they were out of sight, so he come aboard. He says, "I was listenin' to all de talk. I slips into de river an' was goin' to shove for shore if dey come aboard. Den I was goin' to swim back to de raft when dey was gone. Lord, how you fooled 'em, Huck! Dat was de smartes' dodge!"

Then we talked about the money. It was a good haul: twenty dollars apiece. Jim said we could take deck passage on a steamboat now, and the money would last us as far as we wanted to go in the free states. He said twenty mile more warn't far for the raft to go, but he wished we was already there.

Towards daybreak we tied up, and Jim was mighty particular about hiding the raft good. Then he worked all day fixing things in bundles and getting ready to quit rafting.

About ten that night we came in sight of the lights of a town away down in a left-hand bend. I went off in the canoe to ask about it. Pretty soon I found a man out in the river with a skiff. I ranged up and says, "Mister, is that town Cairo?"

"Cairo? You must be a blame fool."

"What town *is* it?"

"If you want to know, go and find out. If you bother me half a minute more, you'll get something you won't want."

I paddled to the raft. Jim was awful disappointed. I said, "Never mind. I reckon Cairo will be the next place."

We passed another town before daylight, but it was high ground, so I didn't go to shore.

"No high ground around Cairo," Jim says.

We laid up for the day, on a sandbar tolerable close to the left-hand bank. I begun to suspicion something. So did Jim.

I says, "Maybe we went past Cairo in the fog that night."

"Let's not talk about it, Huck. Poor niggers don' have no luck."

When it was daylight, we saw clearer water, from the Ohio, on the east-most part of the river. The rest of the river was the Mississippi's regular muddy water. That told us we'd passed the place where the Ohio and the Mississippi join. We'd missed Cairo, just as we'd feared.

We talked it all over. It wouldn't do to take to the shore because we couldn't take the raft upstream. There warn't no way but to wait for dark, start back in the canoe, and take our chances.

We slept all day in a cottonwood thicket, to be fresh for the work of paddling upstream. When we went back to the raft about dark, the canoe was gone!

We didn't say a word for a good while. By and by, we talked about what we better do. We found there warn't nothin' to do but go on down with the raft 'til we got a chance to buy a canoe to go back in. We wouldn't borrow one when there warn't anybody around because that might set people after us.

After dark we shoved out on the raft. The place to buy canoes is off of rafts laying up at shore. But we didn't see no rafts laying up, so we went along more than three hours.

The night got gray and thick, which is the next meanest thing to fog. You can't tell the river's shape, and you can't see no distance. It got to be very late and still. Then along comes a steamboat up the river. We lit the lantern and judged that she would see it. Upstream boats didn't generally come close to us. They go out and follow the sandbars and hunt for easy water under the reefs. But nights like this they bull right up the channel against the whole river.

We could hear the steamboat pounding along,

but we didn't see her good 'til she was close. She was headed right for us. She was a big one, and she was coming in a hurry, too. She looked like a black cloud with rows of fireflies around it. All of a sudden she bulged out, big and scary, with a long row of wide-open furnace doors shining like red-hot teeth.

There was a yell at us, a jingling of bells to stop the engines, a lot of cussing, and whistling of steam. As Jim dived off one side of the raft and I dived off the other, the steamboat hit the raft.

I dived as deep as I could because the steamboat's thirty-foot wheel had to go over me. I wanted it to have plenty of room. I always been able to stay underwater for a minute. This time I reckon I stayed under a minute and a half. Then, nearly busting, I bounced up for air. I popped out to my armpits, blowed water out of my nose, and puffed a bit. There was a booming current. The steamboat already had started her engines back up. She churned along up the river, out of sight in the thick weather.

I called out for Jim about a dozen times. No answer. I grabbed a plank that touched me while I was treading water and struck out for shore, shoving the plank ahead of me. Every so often I called out for Jim. Then I saw that the current's drift was towards the left-hand shore. That meant that I was in a crossing, so I changed and went that way. It was one of those long, slanting two-mile crossings, so I was a good long time in getting over, especially 'cause it took some of my strength to keep calling for Jim. He never answered.

I made a safe landing and clumb up the bank. I waited on the bank, hoping that Jim would come. I feared he was drownded. I was giving up hope when I seen someone swimming towards me. It was Jim!

Jim come ashore, and we laughed and hugged each other. We was mighty glad to be together again.

We took cover in a thicket of trees, where no one would see us, and plopped down, dead tired. After Jim caught his breath, I asked him how he found me.

He said he swum along behind me and heard me yell every time. He said he didn't answer because he didn't want nobody to pick him up and take him into slavery again. "I got hurt a little an' couldn' swim fast, so I was a considerable ways behin' you towards de last. When you landed, I reckoned I could catch up wid you on land widdout havin' to shout."

"What will we do now, Jim?"

"I got de raft."

"What? Warn't she smashed to pieces?"

"No. Dere warn't no great harm done. If we hadn' dived so deep an' swum so far underwater, an' de night hadn' been so dark, we'd 've seen de raft."

"But how did you get hold of her, Jim? Did you catch her?"

"No. I saw her catched on a snag along here in de bend. I hid her amongst some willows."

When we was rested, we headed for the raft. We jumped aboard and soon was back in the middle of the Mississippi. We felt we was back home. We felt mighty free and comfortable on the raft.

Chapter 12

Three days and nights went by. I could say they swum by because they slid along so quiet, smooth, and lovely. The Mississippi was monstrous big where we was—sometimes a mile and a half wide. We traveled nights and laid up and hid daytimes. As soon as night was almost gone, we stopped navigating and tied up, nearly always in the calm water under a sandbar. We cut young cottonwoods and willows and hid the raft with them. Then we set out the fishing lines. Next we slid into the river and had a swim, to freshen up and cool off. Then we set down on the sandy bottom, where the water was about knee deep, and watched the daylight come. There warn't a sound anywheres, only sometimes the "ribbit" sound that bullfrogs make.

The first thing you see, looking away over the water, is a kind of dull line. That's the woods on the other side. You can't make out nothing else. Then there's a pale place in the sky. Then more paleness spreads around. Then the river softens up away off and isn't black anymore, but gray. You can see little dark spots drifting along far away: trading boats and such. And you can see black streaks: rafts. Sometimes you hear an oar screaking or jumbled-up voices. It's so still, and sounds come so far. By and by, you see the mist curl up off of the water. The east reddens up, and so does the river. You make out a log cabin on the edge of the woods, away on the bank on the river's other side. Then a nice breeze springs up and comes fanning you—cool, fresh, and sweet-smelling on account of the woods and flowers. Next it's full day, with everything smiling in the sun and the songbirds singing away.

A little smoke couldn't be noticed now, so we'd take some fish off the lines and cook up a hot breakfast. Afterwards we'd watch the lonesomeness of the river. By and by, we'd lazy off to sleep. Sometimes we'd wake up when a steamboat went coughing upstream, far off towards the other side. Then for about an hour there wouldn't be nothing to see or hear, just solid lonesomeness. Next we'd see a raft sliding by, away off yonder. So we'd put in the day, lazying around, listening to the stillness.

Once, there was a thick fog. The rafts that went by was beating tin pans so that steamboats wouldn't run over them. A boat or raft went by so close that we could hear them talking, cussing, and laughing. We heard them plain, but we couldn't see no sign of them. It made you feel crawly. It was like spirits talking in the air.

Soon as it was night, we shoved off. When we got the raft out to about the middle of the river, we let her float wherever the current wanted her to. Then we lit the pipes, dangled our legs in the water, and talked about all kinds of things.

Sometimes we had that whole river all to ourselves for the longest time. Yonder, across the water, was the banks and the islands—and maybe a spark, which was a candle in a cabin window. Sometimes we'd see a spark or two on the water, on a raft or skiff. And maybe we'd hear a fiddle tune or a song coming over from one of the crafts.

It's lovely to live on a raft. We had the sky up there, all speckled with stars. We laid on our backs and looked up at them. We discussed whether they was made or only happened. Jim reckoned they was made, but I reckoned they just happened. I judged it would've took too long to make so many.

Once or twice a night, we'd see a steamboat slipping along in the dark. Now and then she'd belch sparks out of her chimneys, and they'd rain down in the river and look awful pretty. Then she'd turn a corner, and her lights would wink out and her noise would shut off and leave the river still again. A long time after she was gone, her waves would reach us and joggle the raft a bit.

After midnight the people on shore went to bed. Then for two or three hours the shores was black—no more sparks in the cabin windows. The sparks was our clock. The first one that showed again meant morning was coming, so we'd hunt a place to hide and tie up right away.

Chapter 13

One morning about daybreak, I found a canoe and crossed over to the main shore. I paddled about a mile up a creek amongst cypress woods, to see if I could get some berries.

Suddenly two men come running up to the edge of the creek. I was about to paddle past as fast as I could, but they called out, "Help! Help!" They said they was being chased by dogs and by men on horseback. They wanted to jump into the canoe.

I says, "I don't hear the dogs or horses yet. You've got time to go through the brush and get up the creek a little ways. Do that. Then take to the water, wade down to me, and get in. That'll throw the dogs off the scent."

They done as I said. As soon as they was aboard, I lit out for our sandbar. In about five minutes we heard the dogs barking and the men shouting, away off. We heard them come along towards the creek but couldn't see them. They seemed to stop awhile. When we got further away, we couldn't hardly hear them. By the time we left a mile of woods behind us and reached the river, everything was quiet. We paddled over to the sandbar and hid in the cottonwoods.

One of the two men was about seventy years old. He had a bald head and gray whiskers. He wore an old, battered slouch hat; a greasy blue wool shirt; ragged blue jeans stuffed into his boots; and one home-knit suspender. An old, long-tailed blue denim coat with slick brass buttons was flung over his arm. He said his name was Alexander Blodgett.

The other fellow was about thirty and dressed just as ornery. He said he was Timothy Bridgewater.

Each man carried a big, ratty-looking carpetbag. Turned out, they didn't know each other.

"What got you into trouble?" Blodgett says to Bridgewater.

"I've been selling something to take plaque off of teeth. It does take it off, though it generally takes the enamel along with it. I stayed one night longer than I should've and was just sliding out when I ran across you on the trail. You told me they were coming for you. I was expecting trouble myself, so I figured I'd put on speed, too. What about *you*?"

"I ran a temperance revival for about a week. I was the pet of the women folks 'cause I was makin' it mighty warm for the rummies. I was takin' in five or six dollars a night—ten cents a head, children and niggers free. Business was growin' all the time. Then a report got around last night that I drink on the sly. A nigger rousted me out this mornin' and told me the people was gatherin' on the quiet with their dogs and horses. He said if they got me, they'd tar and feather me. I lit right out."

"Blodgett, why don't we team up?"

"That's all right with me. What's your main line of business?"

"I'm a printer by trade. I also sell medicines, do theater acting and hypnotizing, teach singing and geography . . . I do almost anything so long as it ain't work. And *you*?"

"I do doctoring and preaching," Blodgett says, "and fortunetelling when I have someone to find out the facts for me."

As soon as we went to the raft and they saw Jim, they asked us a considerable lot of questions. They wanted to know why we covered up the raft and laid by in the daytime instead of traveling. They asked if Jim was a runaway nigger.

"Goodness sakes!" I says. "Would a runaway nigger run *south*?"

They allowed that he wouldn't.

"I'm from Missouri," I says. "My ma's been dead a number of years, and my pa died a little while ago. I'm headed to my Uncle Ben, who's got a little one-horse place on the river, forty-four mile below New Orleans. I ain't got nothin' in the world but this raft and my nigger, Jim. When I was traveling daytimes, I had considerable trouble. People was always coming out in skiffs and trying to take Jim away from me, saying they believed he was a runaway nigger. So we don't travel daytimes no more. Nights people don't bother us."

Bridgewater says, "I'll figure out a way for us to travel in the daytime."

Towards night it begun to darken and look like rain. Heat lightning squirted around low in the sky, and the leaves was beginning to shiver. It was going to be pretty ugly; that was easy to see.

Blodgett and Bridgewater looked at the beds in the wigwam. My bed was a cloth case stuffed with straw. It was better than Jim's, which was stuffed with corn husks. There's always cobs around in a corn-husk bed, and they poke into you. And when you roll over dry husks, it sounds like you was rolling over a pile of dead leaves; it makes such a rustling that you wake up. Bridgewater said he'd take my bed, but Blodgett says, "No, you won't. I'm older than you. You'll take the corn-husk bed." Bridgewater grumbled but went along with that.

We got away as soon as it was good and dark. Blodgett told us to stand well out towards the middle of the river and not show a light 'til we got a long ways below the town. By and by, we come in sight of a little bunch of lights. That was the town. We slid by, about half a mile out. When we was three-quarters of a mile below, we hoisted up our signal lantern.

About ten o'clock it begun to rain, blow, thunder, and lighten. Blodgett told Jim and me to stay on watch 'til the weather got better. Blodgett and Bridgewater crawled into the wigwam and turned in for the night.

It was my watch first, but I wouldn't 've turned in even if I'd had a bed—because a body don't see such a storm every day in the week, not by a long sight. The wind screamed along. Every second or two, there come a glare that lit up the whitecaps for half a mile around. You'd see islands looking dusty through the rain, and trees thrashing around in the wind. Then comes a whack! boom! and the thunder goes rumbling away and quits. Then—rip!—comes another flash and another boom. Sometimes the waves almost washed me off the raft, but I didn't mind. We didn't have no trouble with snags. The lightning glared and flittered around so constant that we could see them plenty soon enough to throw the raft's head this way or that and miss them.

By the middle of my watch, I was pretty sleepy, so Jim said he'd stand the rest of it for me. He was always mighty good that way.

I crawled into the wigwam, but Blodgett and Bridgewater had their legs sprawled around so there warn't no room for me. So I laid outside. I didn't mind the rain because it was warm and the waves warn't running so high now.

About two o'clock they come up again. Jim was going to wake me, but he changed his mind because he reckoned they warn't high enough to do any harm. All of a sudden along comes a ripper and washes me overboard. Jim laughed so hard that he almost couldn't catch his breath.

I took the watch, and Jim laid down and snored away. By and by, the storm let up for good and all. When the first cabin light showed, I rousted Jim, and we slid the raft into hiding quarters for the day.

After breakfast Bridgewater told Blodgett that they could make some money giving a show.

"I'm for anything that pays, Bridgewater, but I don't know nothin' about givin' a show."

"There won't be hardly nothing to it," Bridgewater says. Then they talked together in low voices.

There was a little town about three mile down the bend. After lunch Bridgewater said he'd figured out how we could travel in daylight without it being dangersome for Jim. He said he needed to go down to the town to print something. Blodgett said he'd go, too. We was out of coffee, so Jim said that I better go along with them in the canoe and get some.

When we got to the town, there warn't nobody around. We found a sick nigger sunning himself in a backyard. He said almost everybody was gone to a camp meeting, about two mile back in the woods. Bridgewater asked for directions to the town's printing office.

When we got to the printing office, the doors was unlocked and nobody was around. It was a dirty, littered-up place. The walls had handbills with pictures of runaway niggers. Bridgewater set up and printed a picture of a runaway nigger with a bundle on a stick over his shoulder. Below the picture it said, "$200 Reward." The reading was all about Jim. It described him to a dot. It said he run away from Jacque's Plantation, forty mile below New Orleans, last winter and likely went north. It said whoever catched him and sent him back could have the reward and expenses.

Bridgewater says, "Now we can travel in the daytime if we want to. Whenever we see anybody coming, we can tie Jim hand and foot with a rope, lay him in the wigwam, and show this handbill. We'll say we captured him up the river and were too poor to travel on a steamboat, so we rented this little raft and are going down to get the reward."

Blodgett and me said Bridgewater was pretty smart.

When we got back to the raft, we kept still 'til nearly ten o'clock at night. Then we shoved off. We didn't hoist our lantern 'til we was clear out of sight of the town.

Chapter 14

After sunup we went right on and didn't tie up. When we come in sight of a little town in a big bend, we tied up about three-quarters of a mile above it, in the mouth of a creek bordered by cypress trees. Bridgewater, Blodgett, and me took the canoe and went down to arrange for the show. We left Jim all tied up, in the wigwam, so that he'd look captured if anybody happened on to him.

Bridgewater rented the courthouse for that night. Then he got some big sheets of wrapping paper and some black paint and writ advertisements for the show. They read: "At the Courthouse! A Great Show! 3 Nights Only! Admission: 50 cents." At the bottom was the biggest line of all: "LADIES AND CHILDREN NOT ADMITTED."

"There," Bridgewater says. "That'll fetch 'em."

We stuck up the ads all over the town. It was a rundown place. All the streets was just mud—as black as tar, about a foot deep in some places and at least a couple of inches deep in all places. Hogs grunted and loafed around everywheres. The stores and houses was mostly old shacks that hadn't ever been painted. They was set up three or four foot above ground on stilts, to be out of reach of water when the river overflowed. All the stores was along one street. They had awnings in front, and people hitched their horses to the awning posts. Every awning post had a loafer leaning against it. He almost always had his hands in his pants pockets, except when he fetched them out to lend someone a chew of tobacco or to scratch himself. There was empty dry-goods boxes under the awnings, and more loafers sat on them. They whittled, chewed tobacco, yawned, and stretched. The men generally had on yellow straw hats almost as wide as umbrellas. They didn't wear no coats nor waistcoats. They called each other Buck, Hank, Andy, and Joe. They talked with a lazy drawl and used considerable many cuss words.

That night at the courthouse, Blodgett and Bridgewater rigged up a stage, a curtain, and a row of candles for footlights. The house was jam full of men in no time. When no one else come, Bridgewater quit tending the door. He went up on the stage, stood before the curtain, and said that people was about to see a thrilling spectacle. Then he rolled up the curtain. The next minute Blodgett come prancing out on all fours, naked. He was painted all over with different color stripes. The people almost killed themselves laughing. When Blodgett finished prancing around, he went behind the scenes. The people roared, clapped, and haw-hawed 'til he come back and done it again.

Then Bridgewater lets the curtain down, bows to the people, and says the show will be performed only two more nights. Then he bows again and says that if he has succeeded in pleasing them, they should please tell their friends to come see the show.

Twenty people calls out, "What? Is it over? Is that *all*?"

Bridgewater says yes. Then everybody calls out, "We've been swindled!" They rose up, mad, and started goin' for Bridgewater.

But a big man jumps up on a bench and shouts, "Hold on!" Everybody stopped to listen. "We've been swindled, but we don't want to be the laughingstocks of this town and never hear the end of this. No. What we should do is go out of here quiet and talk up this show. Sell the rest of the town on it. Then we'll all be in the same boat."

"He's right," everybody says.

"All right, then. Not a word about any swindle. Go home, and tell everybody to come see the show."

The next night, the house was jammed. Bridgewater swindled the crowd the same way as he done before.

About midnight Bridgewater and Blodgett made Jim and me back the raft out, float her down the middle of the river, and fetch her in and hide her about two mile below town.

The third night the house was jammed again. There warn't newcomers this time but people that was at the show one of the other two nights. I stood by Bridgewater at the door, and I see that every man that went in had his pockets bulging or something muffled up under his coat. I smelt sickly eggs by the barrel, and rotten cabbages, and such things. When the place couldn't hold no more people, Bridgewater give a fellow a quarter and told him to tend the door for him a minute. Then Bridgewater and me started around for the back door. The minute we turned the corner and was in the dark, Bridgewater says, "Walk fast 'til you get away from the houses. Then run for the raft as fast as you can."

I done it, and he done the same. We struck the raft at the same time. In less than two seconds we was gliding downstream, all dark and still. We edged towards the middle of the river, nobody saying a word. I reckoned Blodgett was in for a rough time with the audience. But pretty soon he crawls out from under the wigwam, and says, "Well, how'd it pan out, Bridgewater?" He hadn't been in the town at all.

We never showed a light 'til we was about ten mile below the town. Then we lit up and had a supper. Blodgett and Bridgewater fairly laughed their bones loose over the way they'd fooled them people. Bridgewater says, "Flatheads! I knew that the first audience would keep mum and let the rest of the town get roped in. And I knew that they'd lay for us the third night." Them rascals took in four hundred and sixty-five dollars in those three nights. I never seen money hauled in by the wagonload like that before.

When they was asleep and snoring, Jim says, "Huck, don' it bother you de way dey carries on? Dey's reg'lar scoundrels."

"I feel the same way, Jim, but it seems too dangersome to try and unload them."

I went to sleep, and Jim didn't call me when it was my turn. He often done that.

When I waked up just at daybreak, Jim was sitting with his head down between his knees, moaning and mourning to himself. I knowed he was thinking about his wife and children, away up yonder. He was low and homesick for them. He hadn't ever been away from them before in his life. I believe he cared just as much for *his* people as white folks does for *theirs*. He often moaned and mourned that way nights, when he judged I was asleep. He'd say, "Poor 'Lizabeth. Poor Johnny. I expec' I ain't ever goin' to see you no more." Jim was a mighty good nigger.

This time I got to talking to him about his wife and young ones.

Jim says, "I heard somethin' over yonder on de bank like a whack or a slam, an' it remin' me o' de time I treat my little 'Lizabeth so bad. She warn't only about four year old. She got de scarlet fever an' had a powerful rough spell. But she got through it. One day, she was standin' around an' I says to her, 'Shut de door.' She didn' do it—just stood dere smilin' up at me. I got mad and says loud, 'I said to shut de door!' She just stood de same way. I says, 'I'll make you mind!' An' I fetched her a slap on de side o' her head dat sent her sprawling. Den I went into de other room for a minute. When I come back, de door still was standin' open. 'Lizabeth was lookin' down, and tears was runnin' down her face. Just den, along come de wind an' slam de door shut—blam!—right behin' de chil'. An'—my Lord—she never moved. My breath almost hopped out o' me, an' I started tremblin'. I went aroun' behin' her and yells 'Pow!' as loud as I could. She never budge. Oh, Huck! I bust out cryin', grab her up in my arms, and says, "Lizabeth! 'Lizabeth! Lord forgive me, 'cause I ain't never goin' to forgive *myself*!" She was plumb deaf an' dumb, Huck. Plumb deaf an' dumb. An' I'd been treatin' her so!"

Chapter 15

For days we kept right along down the river. We was down south in the warm weather now and a mighty long ways from home. We begun to come to trees with Spanish moss on them, hanging down from the limbs like long, gray beards. It was the first I ever seen, and it made the woods look solemn and dismal.

Bridgewater and Blodgett wanted to do the show again, but they reckoned it was too risky. Word might've worked its way down to other towns. So they tried other ways of cheating people: missionarying, hypnotizing, and telling fortunes. But they didn't make much money. Finally they begun to lay their heads together in the wigwam and talk low and secret-like. Jim and me got uneasy. We judged they was studying up some worse deviltry than ever. Jim and me feared they was planning to break into somebody's house or store. That scared us. We agreed that we wouldn't have nothing to do with such actions. We also said that if we got the chance, we'd clear out and leave them scoundrels behind.

Early one morning we hid the raft in a good, safe place about two mile below a shabby little town. Blodgett went ashore and told us all to stay hid while he went up to town and smelt around to see if anybody had got wind of the phony show yet. He said if he warn't back by midday, Bridgewater and me would know it was all right and should come help him set up.

When midday come, Bridgewater and me went up to the town and hunted around for Blodgett. We found him in the back room of a tavern, so drunk he couldn't walk. Bridgewater called him an old fool, and they started to argue.

I lit out and bounded down the river road like a deer. This was the chance that Jim and me had waited for. I didn't want to ever see them scoundrels again.

I reached the raft all out of breath but loaded up with joy. I called, "We're rid of 'em, Jim!" I hurried into the wigwam. Jim warn't there! I called out, but there warn't no answer. I run this way and that in the woods, calling for Jim. Then I set down and cried.

I couldn't set still long, though. I went out on the road, trying to think what I should do. I run across a boy walking along and asked him if he'd heard anything about somebody finding a nigger.

"Yes," he says. "They've got him down at Silas

Phelps's place, two mile below here. He run off from down south somewheres. There's a two-hundred-dollar reward for him."

"Who turned him in?"

"An old fellow, a stranger. He sold him for only forty dollars because he's got to go up the river and can't wait. *I'd* wait, you bet."

"Maybe he sold the nigger for so little 'cause something ain't straight about it."

"No, it's straight as a string. I seen the hand-bill myself. It tells all about the nigger and paints him like a picture. It says he's from a plantation below New Orleans."

I went to the raft and set down in the wigwam to think. Everything was ruined because of those scoundrels. They was mighty low to go back on Jim and make him a slave again all his life— amongst strangers, too. And all for forty dirty dol-lars. I said to myself that if Jim had to be a slave, it would be a thousand times better for him to be a slave at home where his family was. So I decided to write a letter to Miss Watson and tell her where Jim was.

But I soon give up that notion because she'd be mad at Jim for his rascality and ungratefulness to her. She'd sell him straight down the river. If she didn't, everybody would despise Jim for being ungrateful. They'd make him feel it all the time. And it would get around that I'd helped a nigger try to get his freedom. If I ever saw anybody from

St. Petersburg again, I'd have to get down and lick their boots for shame.

I'd done a low-down thing, but I'd been fine with it as long as I could hide it. The more I thought about this, the more my conscience went to grinding me, and the more wicked I got to feeling. Suddenly it hit me: here was the plain hand of God slapping me in the face and letting me know that my wickedness was being watched all the time from up there in Heaven. I'd stole the nigger of a poor old woman that hadn't ever done me no harm. Now God was showing me that He always is on the lookout and that He'll allow such miserable doings to go only so far and no farther. I was so scared that I almost dropped in my tracks. I tried the best I could to soften it up for myself by saying that I was brung up wicked, so I warn't really to blame. But something inside of me kept saying, "You could've gone to Sunday school. They would've learnt you that people that acts like *you* been acting about that nigger goes to everlasting fire."

It made me shiver. I made up my mind to pray and see if I could try to quit being the kind of boy I was and be better. I kneeled down. But the words wouldn't come. It warn't no use to try and hide it from Him. Nor from myself, neither. The words wouldn't come because my heart warn't right. I was letting on to give up sin, but inside of me I was holding on to the biggest one of all. I was trying to make my mouth say that I would do the right thing—go and write to Jim's owner and tell where he was. But deep down in me, I knowed it was a lie. And God knowed it. You can't pray a lie. I found that out.

So I was full of trouble and didn't know what to do. At last I had an idea. I thinks, "I'll go and write the letter and then see if I can pray. It was astonishing; right away I felt a thousand times better. So I got a piece of paper and a pencil and set down and wrote:

> Miss Watson, your runaway nigger Jim is down here two mile below Pikesville. Mr. Phelps has got him. He will give Jim up for the reward if you send.
>
> Huck Finn

I felt washed clean of sin. I knowed I could pray now, but I didn't do it straight off. I laid the paper down and set there thinking—thinking how good it was that Jim was captured and how near I come to going to Hell.

Then I got to thinking about our trip down the river. I'd see Jim before me, in the day and in the nighttime—sometimes in storms—and us floating along, talking, singing, and laughing. I couldn't think of no things to harden me against him, but only the other kind. I'd see him standing my watch on top of his, so I could go on sleeping. I remembered how glad he was when I come back out of the fog and how good he always was. I remembered the time that I saved him by telling the men that my pa had smallpox. Jim was so grateful and said that I was the best friend he ever had.

I looked at the letter. I took it up and held it in my hand. I was trembling. I had to decide, forever, between two things. I thought a minute, sort of holding my breath. Then I says, "All right, then. I'll go to Hell." And I tore it up.

It was awful words, but they was said, and I let them *stay* said. I didn't think no more about reforming. I would stick to wickedness. That was in my line 'cause I was brung up to it, and goodness warn't. For a starter, I'd go to work and steal Jim out of slavery again. And if I could think up anything worse, I'd do *that*—because as long as I was in, and in for good, I might as well go the whole hog.

Then I set to thinking over how to free Jim. At last I fixed on a plan that suited me.

There was a woody island down the river a piece. As soon as it was fairly dark, I crept out with my raft and went for it. I hid my raft there and went to sleep.

I got up before it was light, had my breakfast, put on my best clothes, tied up some things in a bundle, took the canoe, and cleared for shore. I landed below where I judged Phelps's place was and hid my bundle in the woods. Then I loaded the canoe with rocks and sunk her where I could find her again when I wanted her, about a quarter of a mile below a little sawmill on the bank.

Then I struck up the road. When I passed the sawmill, I seen a sign on it: "Phelps's Sawmill." When I come to the farmhouses, two or three hundred yards further along, I kept my eyes peeled. I didn't see nobody, though it was good daylight now. I shoved along, straight for town.

The very first man I seen when I got there was Bridgewater. He was sticking up an ad for his show. He saw me before I could hide.

He looked astonished and says, "Where'd *you* come from?" Then he says, all eager, "Where's the raft? Got her in a good place?"

"That's just what I was going to ask *you*."

He looked disappointed and says, "What are you asking *me* for?"

I says, "Well, when I seen Blodgett so drunk yesterday, I says to myself, 'We can't get him back to the raft for hours, 'til he's soberer.' So I went loafing around town to put in the time and wait. When I got back to the raft, she was gone. So I says to myself, 'They've got into trouble and had to leave. And they've took my nigger, the only one I've got in the world. Now I'm in a strange place and ain't got no property no more, nor nothing.' So I set down and cried. I slept in the woods all night. What *did* become of the raft, then—and Jim?"

"Blamed if I know what become of the raft. As

for Jim—Blodgett sold him for forty dollars."

"Sold him! He was *my* nigger. I want my nigger! And that's *my* forty dollars."

"It's gone. Blodgett gambled away most of it and spent the rest on whisky. When I got him home late last night and found the raft gone, and us flat broke, there warn't nothin' to do but try the show again."

"Where's my nigger?" I says.

"A farmer by the name of Silas Ph . . ." Then he stopped. "Foster. Silas Foster bought him. He lives forty mile back here in the country, on the road to Lafayette."

I figured he was lying 'cause he didn't want me to make no trouble for him and Blodgett. "All right," I says. "I can walk it in three days."

"Well, clear out."

I left. I felt Bridgewater was watching me, so I went straight out in the country as much as a mile before I stopped. Then I doubled back through the woods towards Phelps's.

Chapter 16

When I got to the Phelps farm, it was Sunday-like—all still except for the faint dronings of bugs and flies. The hands was gone to the fields. It was hot and sunshiny.

Phelps's place was a little cotton plantation like every other. It had a rail fence around a two-acre yard. The yard had some sickly patches of grass, but mostly it was bare and smooth, like an old hat with the nap rubbed off. There was a big log house for the white folks. The chinks between the logs was stopped with mud that had been whitewashed some time or other. An open but roofed passage joined the kitchen to the rest of the house. Back of the kitchen was a log smokehouse. Near the smokehouse was three little nigger cabins in a row. There was some outbuildings down a piece. There was one little cabin all by itself away down against the back fence. Near the cabin was a big kettle to boil soap in. Hounds was sleeping in different places. There was three shade trees off in a corner, some berry bushes in one place by the fence, and a garden and watermelon patch outside the fence. Then the cotton fields began. After the fields was the woods.

I started for the kitchen. When I got a little ways, I heard the dim hum of a spinning wheel. I went right along, not with any particular plan. I just trusted that the right words would come when I needed them. When I got half way, one hound and then another got up. In a quarter of a minute I was surrounded by fifteen of them. They stretched their necks and noses up towards me, barking and howling. More was coming. They was sailing over fences and around corners from everywheres.

A nigger woman come tearing out of the kitchen. She called out, "That's enough, Tige! Spot! That's enough!" The dogs started wagging their tails around me and making friends with me. There ain't no harm in a hound.

Behind the woman comes a little nigger girl and two little nigger boys without anything on but linen shirts. They hung onto their mother's dress and peeped out at me, bashful, from behind her skirt.

Then a white woman come running from the house. She was about fifty year old and bareheaded. She had a spinning stick in her hand. Behind her comes her little children. I figured she was Mrs. Phelps. She was smiling all over. She cries,

"Tom! It's you at last!"

Without thinking, I says, "Yes, ma'am."

She grabbed me and hugged me tight. "Goodness, I'm glad to see you! You don't look as much like your mother as I reckoned you would. Children, it's your cousin Tom! Tell him howdy." But they hid behind her. "Lize, hurry up and get him a hot breakfast. Or did you get breakfast on the boat?"

I said I'd got it on the boat.

Mrs. Phelps started for the house, leading me by the hand, and the children tagging after. When we got there, she set me down in a chair and set herself down on a low stool in front of me. She held both my hands and says, "Now I can have a good look at you. I've been hungry for it for years. We was expecting you a few days ago. What kept you? Boat go aground?"

"Yes, ma'am. She . . ."

"Don't say 'ma'am.' Say 'Aunt Sally.' Where'd she go aground?"

I didn't know what to say because I didn't know whether the boat would be coming up the river or down. So I says, "It warn't the grounding that kept us. We blowed out a cylinder head."

"Good gracious! Anybody hurt?"

"No, ma'am. Killed a nigger."

"Well, it's lucky because sometimes people do get hurt. Two years ago last Christmas, your Uncle Silas was coming up from New Orleans on a steamboat, and she blowed out a cylinder head. It crippled a man, and I think he died afterwards. Your Uncle Silas knowed a family in Baton Rouge that knowed his people. Yes, I remember now. He *did* die. They amputated his leg, but it didn't save him. He turned blue all over and died. Your uncle's been up to the town every day to fetch you. He went again not more than an hour ago. He'll be back any minute now. Where's your baggage?"

"I left it near the wharf. Forgot it."

"Why, it'll be stole!"

"No, it's somewheres safe." I was uneasy. I wanted to get the children over to one side and pump them a little, to find out who I was.

"How's Sis and everyone else? Tell me all about them—how they are, what they been doing."

I see I was up a stump and up it good. I says to myself, "I got to risk the truth." I opened my mouth to begin.

But Mrs. Phelps grabbed me and hustled me behind the bed. "Here he comes! Stick your head down lower, so you can't be seen. Don't let on that you're here. Children, don't say a word."

There warn't nothing I could do but just hold still. I had one little glimpse of Mr. Phelps when he come in. Then the bed hid him.

Mrs. Phelps jumps for him and says, "Has he come?"

"No," her husband says.

"Goodness gracious!" she says. "What in the world can have become of him?"

"I don't know," Mr. Phelps says. "It makes me dreadful uneasy. Something must've happened to the boat."

"Silas, look yonder, up the road! Ain't that somebody coming?"

He sprung to the window at the head of the bed. That give Mrs. Phelps the chance that she wanted. She stooped down quick at the foot of the bed and give me a pull. Out I come. When Mr. Phelps turned back from the window, there she stood beaming like a house on fire. I stood meek and sweaty alongside.

The old gentleman stared. "Why, who's *that*?"

"Who do you *reckon* it is?"

"I ain't got no idea. Who *is* it?"

"Tom Sawyer!"

By jings, I almost slumped through the floor! Mr. Phelps grabbed me by the hand and kept shaking it. All the time, Mrs. Phelps danced around, laughing.

Then how they both did fire off questions about Tom's family.

But if they was joyful, it warn't nothing to what *I* was. I was so glad to find out who I was!

They froze to me for two hours. I told them more about the Sawyer family than ever happened to any six Sawyer families. At last, my chin was so tired that it couldn't hardly go anymore. Being Tom Sawyer was easy and comfortable, and it stayed easy and comfortable 'til I hear a steamboat coughing down the river. Then I thinks, "Suppose Tom's on that boat. Suppose he steps in here and sings out my name before I can throw him a wink to keep quiet." I couldn't have that happen, so I decided to go up the road and waylay him. I told the folks I reckoned I'd fetch my baggage. Mr. Phelps was for going along with me, but I said no. I said that I could drive the horse myself, and I'd rather he didn't take no trouble about me.

Chapter 17

I started off in the wagon. When I was half way, I see a wagon coming. Sure enough, it was Tom Sawyer. I stopped and waited 'til he come along.

I says, "Hold on!"

Tom's wagon stopped alongside, and his mouth opened up like a trunk and stayed that way. He swallowed a few times, like a person that's got a dry throat. Then he says, "I ain't ever done you no harm. You know that. So, what do you want to come back and haunt me for?"

"I ain't come back," I says. "I ain't been gone."

When Tom heard my voice, it righted him up some. But he warn't satisfied yet. "Don't you play nothing on me because I wouldn't on *you*. You ain't a ghost?"

"I ain't a ghost."

"But warn't you murdered?"

"No. I played it on them."

Tom was so glad to see me again that he didn't

know what to do. He wanted to know all about it right off because it was a grand adventure and mysterious.

But I says, "Leave it alone 'til by and by." I told his driver to wait, and we drove off a little piece. I told Tom the fix I was in. "What do you reckon we better do?"

Tom thought and thought. Pretty soon he says, "I've got it. Take my trunk in your wagon, and let on it's yours. Turn back and fool along slow, so as to get to the house about the time you ought to. I'll go towards town a piece, take a fresh start, and get to the house about half an hour after you. At first, don't let on to know me."

"All right. But there's one more thing—something that nobody don't know but me. There's a nigger here that I'm trying to steal out of slavery. It's Jim—Miss Watson's Jim."

"What? Why, Jim is . . ." Tom stopped and went to thinking.

"I know what you'll say. You'll say it's a dirty, low-down business. Well, what if it *is*? *I'm* low-down. I'm going to steal him, and I want you to keep mum. Will you?"

Tom's eyes lit up. "I'll help you steal him!"

Well, I felt like I'd been shot. It was the most astonishing thing I ever heard. Tom Sawyer a nigger stealer! He fell considerable in my estimation. Then I says, "Oh, shucks. You're joking."

"I ain't joking."

"Well, joking or no joking, if you hear any- thing about a runaway nigger, don't forget to remember that you don't know nothing about him, and *I* don't know nothing about him."

We took Tom's trunk and put it in my wagon. Tom drove off his way, and I drove mine. But I forgot all about driving slow on account of being glad and full of thinking, so I got back a heap too quick for the length of the trip.

Mr. Phelps was at the door. He says, "Why, this is wonderful! Whoever would've thought it was in that mare to do it? I wish we'd timed her. And she ain't sweated a hair. Not a hair. Why, I wouldn't take a hundred dollars for that horse now. I would've sold her for only fifteen before; I thought that was all she was worth." That's all he said. He was the innocentest, best old soul I ever see.

In about half an hour Tom's wagon drove up. Mrs. Phelps sees it through the window and says, "Why, somebody's come! I wonder who it is. I do believe it's a stranger." Then she says to her little boy, "Jimmy, run and tell Lize to put on another plate for lunch."

Everybody rushed for the front door because a stranger don't come every year. A stranger causes more excitement than the yellow fever.

Tom was starting for the house, and the wagon was spinning up the road to the town. We was all bunched in the front door. Tom had an audience, and that always made him feel good and got him to throw in a suitable amount of style. He warn't a boy to meeky along up that yard, especially when he was wearing *store* clothes. No, he come calm and important. When he got in front of us, he lifts his hat ever so gracious and dainty, like it was the lid of a box that had butterflies asleep in it and he didn't want to disturb them. He says, "Mr. Archibald Nichols?"

"No, my boy," Mr. Phelps says. "Nichols' place is down three mile more."

Tom looked back over his shoulder for the wagon. "Too late. He's out of sight."

"Yes, he's gone, my boy. Come in, and eat your lunch with us. Then we'll hitch up and take you down to Nichols'."

"Oh, I don't want to trouble you. I'll walk. I don't mind the distance."

"No trouble. It wouldn't be Southern hospitality to let you walk. Come in and eat with us."

"Oh, do," Mrs. Phelps says. "It ain't a bit of trouble. You must stay. It's a long, dusty three mile. We can't let you walk. Besides, I already told 'em to put on another plate when I seen you coming. So you musn't disappoint us. Come right in, and make yourself at home."

Tom thanked them very hearty and come in. He said he was from Hicksville, Ohio and his name was William Thompson. He run on and on, making up stuff about Hicksville and everybody in it.

I was getting nervous, wondering how this was going to help me out of my scrape.

By and by, Tom leaned over and kissed Mrs. Phelps right on the mouth. Then he settled back in his chair, all comfortable, and was going on talking.

But Mrs. Phelps jumped up and wiped off the kiss with the back of her hand. "You fresh puppy!"

Tom looked kind of humble and says, "I didn't mean no harm. I thought you'd like it."

"Why, you cheeky boy!" She took up her spinning stick, and it looked like she might give Tom a crack with it. "What made you think I'd like it?"

"They told me you would."

"They told you I would? Who's *they*?"

"They all said, 'Kiss her. She'll like it.' But I won't ever do it again—'til you ask me."

"'Til I ask you! Well, I never!"

Then Tom looks at me and says, "Tom, didn't you think that Aunt Sally would throw open her arms and say, 'Sid Sawyer, . . .'"

"My land!" Mrs. Phelps says, breaking in and jumping for him. "You fresh rascal, to fool a body so."

She went to hug him, but he fended her off. "Not 'til you ask me."

She asked him. Then she hugged and kissed him over and over. Then she turned him over to Mr. Phelps, and he took what was left. After they got a little quiet again, Mrs. Phelps says, "Dear me, I ain't never seen such a surprise. We warn't expecting you, but only Tom. Sis never wrote to me about anybody coming but Tom."

"That's because it warn't intended for anybody to come but Tom. But I begged and begged. At the last minute Aunt Polly let *me* come, too. Coming down the river, Tom and me thought it would be a first-rate surprise for him to come here to the house first, and for me to drop in by and by and let on to be a stranger."

"You ought to have your jaws boxed. But I'd be willing to stand a thousand such jokes to have you here. Well, to think of that performance! I don't deny it; I was almost froze with astonishment when you give me that kiss."

We had lunch out in the passage between the house and the kitchen. There was food enough on that table for seven families. And all hot, too—none of your flabby, tough meat that's laid in a cupboard in a damp cellar all night and tastes like a hunk of old, cold leather in the morning. Mr. Phelps said a long blessing over the food, but it didn't make the food get cold the way I've seen them long blessings do lots of times.

There was a good deal of talk all afternoon, but they didn't say nothing about any runaway nigger, and Tom and me was afraid to bring it up.

That night, at supper, one of the little boys says, "Pa, can Tom, Sid, and me go to the show?"

"No," Mr. Phelps says. "I reckon there ain't

going to *be* any show. And you couldn't go if there *was*. The runaway nigger told Burton and me all about that scandalous show, and Burton said he'd tell the people. I reckon they've drove those scoundrels out of town by now."

So, Jim was here, all right.

Tom and me was to sleep in the same room and bed. Right after supper we said good night and went up to bed. I didn't like Blodgett and Bridgewater, but it didn't feel right not to warn them. So Tom and me clumb out the window and down the lightning rod and shoved for the town.

On the road Tom told me all about how people reckoned I was murdered. He said Pap disappeared pretty soon after I was killed and didn't come back. He said there was quite a stir when Jim run away.

I told Tom about Blodgett and Bridgewater and as much of the raft voyage as I had time to.

As Tom and me struck into the town, here comes a raging rush of people with torches. They was whooping, yelling, banging tin pans, and blowing horns. We jumped to one side to let them go by. As they went, I seen they had Blodgett and Bridgewater straddling a rail. That is, I *knowed* it was Blodgett and Bridgewater. They was all over tar and feathers and didn't look like nothing human. They looked like a couple of monstrous plumes. They was rascals, but it made me sick to see it. People can be awful cruel to each other.

We asked some stragglers about it, and they said that everybody went to the show and kept quiet 'til Blodgett was in the middle of his cavortings on the stage. Then somebody give a signal, and the house rose up and went for them.

There was nothing we could do, so Tom and me poked along back to the house. I felt to blame, though I hadn't done nothing. That's always the way. It don't make no difference whether you do right or wrong. A person's conscience ain't got no sense and just goes for them anyway. A conscience takes up more room than all the rest of a person's insides, yet it don't do no good. Tom Sawyer says the same.

Chapter 18

Tom and me stopped talking and got to thinking.

By and by, Tom says, "Looky here, Huck. What fools we were not to think of it before! I bet I know where Jim is."

"Where?"

"In that little cabin that's all by itself. When we was at lunch, I saw a nigger man go in there with some food. He unlocked the padlock when he went in, and he locked it again when he come out. He gave Uncle Silas a key about the time that we got up from the table—the key for that padlock, I bet. So that's where Jim is. I'm glad I found it out detective fashion. I wouldn't give shucks for any other way. Work your mind, and figure out a plan to steal Jim. I'll figure out one, too. Then we'll take the one we like best."

I went to thinking out a plan but only just to be doing something; I knowed very well who was going to come up with the best plan.

Pretty soon Tom says, "Ready?"

"Yes."

"All right. What's your plan?"

"We can find out easy if it's Jim in there. Tomorrow we can get my canoe and fetch my raft over from the island. The first dark night, we can steal the key from Mr. Phelps's pants after he goes to bed. We can shove off down the river on the raft with Jim, hiding daytimes and traveling nights, the way Jim and me used to do. Wouldn't that work?"

"Work? Why, certainly it would work. But it's too darn simple. There ain't nothing to it. What's the good of a plan that ain't no more trouble than *that*?"

I never said nothing because I warn't expecting nothing different.

Tom told me his plan, and I see in a minute it was worth fifteen of mine for style. It would make Jim just as free a man as mine would and maybe get us all killed besides. So I was satisfied.

One thing was sure: Tom Sawyer was going to help steal a nigger out of slavery. That was the thing that was too much for me. Here was a boy that was respectable and well brung up. He had a character to lose and folks at home that had characters. He was bright, not leather-headed; knowing, not ignorant; kind, not mean. Yet here he was, without any more pride, rightness, or feeling than to stoop to this business and shame himself and his family, before everybody. I couldn't understand it no way at all. It was outrageous, and I knowed I ought to just up and tell him so. If I was his true friend, I'd tell him to quit this thing right where he was and save himself. So I started to tell him.

But he shut me up. "Don't you reckon I know what I'm doing?"

"Yes."

"Didn't I say I was going to help steal Jim?"

"Yes."

"Well, then."

That's all he said, and that's all *I* said.

When we got back, the house was dark and still. We went down to the little cabin to examine it. We went through the yard, to see what the hounds would do. They knowed us and didn't make no more noise than country dogs always does when something comes by in the night. When we got to the cabin, we took a look at the front and the two sides. On the north side we found a square window-hole, up tolerable high, with one stout board nailed across it.

I says, "Here's the ticket. This hole's big enough for Jim to get through if we wrench off the board."

Tom says, annoyed-like, "That's as simple as playing hooky. We certainly can find a more complicated way than *that*, Huck Finn."

"Well, then," I says, "how will it do to saw him out, the way I done before I was murdered?"

"That's more like it," Tom says. "It's mysterious and troublesome. But I bet we can find a way that's twice as long. Let's keep looking around."

Between the cabin and the fence, on the back side, was a shed that joined the cabin at the eaves. It was made out of planks. The shed was as long as the cabin but narrow—about six foot wide. The door to it was at the south end. It had a chain across it. The chain was fastened by a staple at one end and by a padlock at the other. Tom went to the soap kettle and searched around. He brung back the iron thing they lift the lid with. He took it and pried out the staple. The chain fell down, and we opened the door. We went in, shut the door, and struck a match. We see the shed was only built against the cabin; it hadn't no connection with it. There warn't no floor to the shed, nor nothing in it but a broken plow and some rusty old hoes, spades, and picks. The match went out, and so did we. We shoved the staple back in, and the door was locked as good as ever.

Tom was overjoyed. "We'll dig him out. It'll take about a week!"

In the morning we was up at daybreak and down to the nigger cabins to pet the dogs and make friends with Nat, the nigger that fed Jim—if it *was* Jim that was being fed. The niggers was just getting through breakfast and starting for the fields. Nat was piling up a tin pan with bread, meat, and other food. He had a good-natured face. His hair was all tied up in little bunches with thread. That was to keep witches away. While the other niggers was leaving, the key come from the house.

Tom says, "What's the food for?"

"For de runaway," Nat says.

"We'll take it in," Tom says.

"Are you sure, Maste' Sid?"

"Yes."

When we got in, it was so dark that we couldn't hardly see anything. Sure enough, Jim was there. He could see us. He says, "Huck! An'—good Lord!—ain't dat Miste' Tom?"

Tom told Jim, "Don't ever let on to know us in front of anybody else. And if you hear any digging going on nights, it's us. We're going to set you free."

Jim grabbed our hands and squeezed them.

Then Nat come in. We said we'd come again some time if Nat wanted us to. He said he would, most particular if it was dark because witches come around mostly in the dark, so it's good to have folks around then.

Chapter 19

It would be almost an hour 'til breakfast, so we left. We struck down into the woods because Tom said we got to have some light to dig by, but a lantern makes too much and might get us into trouble. He said what we needed was foxfire, the soft glow that rotting wood gives off in a dark place. We fetched an armful of rotting chunks and hid them in the weeds. Then we set down to rest.

Tom says, kind of dissatisfied, "Blame it, this whole thing is way too easy. It makes it rotten difficult to come up with a difficult plan. There ain't no watchman to be drugged. There ain't even a dog to give a sleeping mixture to. Uncle Silas trusts everybody. He sends the key to Nat and don't send nobody to watch him. And Jim is chained by one leg to the leg of his bed. Why, all you got to do is lift the bed and slip off the chain. Jim could've got out that window-hole by now, only there wouldn't be no use trying to travel with a ten-foot chain on his leg. Drat it, Huck, it's the stupidest arrangement I ever seen. We got to invent all the difficulties. Well, I guess there's more honor getting Jim out when we have to create all the difficulties out of our own heads instead of having them created *for* us. The lantern's a good example. We'll just have to *pretend* that a lantern's risky. The cold, hard truth is that we could work with a torchlight procession if we wanted to." After a pause, Tom says, "We need a saw."

"What do we want with a saw?"

"What do we want with a saw? We got to saw off the leg of Jim's bed, to get his chain loose."

"Why, you just said a body could lift the bed and slip the chain off!"

"Well, ain't that just like you, Huck Finn. Ain't you ever read any books? All the best authorities would say we got to saw the bed-leg in two. Then we swallow the sawdust and put some dirt and grease around the sawed place, so no one can see that the leg was sawed. The night we're ready, we kick the leg and down it goes. Then we slip off the chain. Also, Jim needs a rope ladder. We can tear up our sheets and make him one. And we can send it to him in a pie. It's mostly done that way. And I've ate worse pies than one with sheets in it."

"Tom Sawyer, how you talk! Jim ain't got no use for a rope ladder."

"How *you* talk. Jim's *got* to have a rope ladder. All prisoners do."

"What in the nation can he do with it?"

"He can hide it in his bed. That's what all prisoners do. Then it's there as a clue after Jim's gone. Don't you reckon they'll want clues? Of course, they will. And you wouldn't leave them any?"

"Well," I says, "if Jim's got to have it, I'll borrow a sheet off the clothesline."

That give Tom another idea. "Borrow a shirt, too."

"What do we want a shirt for?"

"Jim will keep a diary on it."

"Diary your granny! Jim can't write."

"So what? He can make marks, can't he?"

"With what?"

"I've got a piece of red chalk. Jim can use that. It'll look like blood. And when Jim wants to send a message to let the world know where he's captivated, he can scratch it on the bottom of a tin plate with a fork and throw the plate out the window."

"Jim ain't got no tin plates. They feed him with a pan."

"We can get him some."

"Can't nobody read any plate he might scratch on."

"That don't matter, Huck Finn."

"What's the sense in wasting the plates?"

Suddenly we heard the breakfast horn blowing and cleared out for the house. It was just as well because Tom looked mighty disgusted with me.

During the morning I borrowed a sheet and a

white shirt off the clothesline. I found an old sack and put them in it. Tom and me went down and got the rotten wood and put that in, too. We waited 'til everybody was settled down to business and nobody was around the yard. Then Tom carried the sack into the shed while I stood off a piece to keep watch. By and by, he come out, and we went and set down on a woodpile to talk.

Tom says, "Everything's all right now except tools."

"Tools for what?"

"Why, to dig with."

"Ain't them old picks and things in there good enough to dig with?"

He turns to me, with a pitying look. "Huck Finn, did you ever hear of a prisoner having picks and shovels to dig himself out with? How can a prisoner be a hero if he has picks and shovels? Why, they might as well give him the key and be done with it."

"Well, what will we dig with, then?"

"A couple of knives."

"We goin' to dig the foundations out from under that cabin with a couple of knifes?"

"Yes."

"Confound it, that's foolish, Tom."

"There ain't no other way that I ever heard of, and I've read all the books that gives any information about these things. They always dig out with a knife. And not through dirt, mind you. Generally it's through solid rock. And it takes them years."

"Jim's too old to be dug out with knifes. He won't last."

"Yes, he will. It won't take so long to dig out through a dirt foundation."

"How long will it take?"

"Well, we can't risk being as long as we ought to because it may not take very long for Uncle Silas to hear from down there by New Orleans. He'll find out that Jim ain't from there. Then he'll advertise Jim, or something like that. So I recommend that we dig as quick as we can. Then we can snatch Jim out and rush him away at the first sign of trouble. We can pretend we dug for thirty-seven years."

"Now, there's sense in that," I says. "Pretending don't cost nothing. I'll go find us a couple of knifes."

"Get three. We'll make a saw out of one of them."

"If it ain't irreligious to suggest it, there's an old rusty saw blade behind the smokehouse."

Tom looked weary and discouraged. "It ain't no use trying to learn you anything, Huck."

Chapter 20

That night, as soon as we reckoned everybody was asleep, we went down the lightning rod and shut ourselves up in the shed. We got our pile of rotten wood and went to work by the glow of the foxfire. We cleared everything out of the way along a five-foot area behind the part of the cabin with Jim's bed. We'd dig in under the bed. When we got through, nobody in the cabin would know there was any hole there because Jim's bedcover hung down almost to the ground. You'd have to raise it and look under to see the hole.

We dug with the knifes 'til almost midnight. Then we was dog tired, and our hands was blistered. Yet, there warn't no hole to speak of.

I says, "This ain't no thirty-seven-year job, Tom Sawyer. This is a thirty-*eight*-year job."

Tom sighed, and pretty soon he stopped digging. "It ain't no use, Huck. It ain't going to work. If we was prisoners, we'd have as many years as we wanted. And our hands wouldn't get blistered because we wouldn't get but a few minutes to dig every day, while the guards was changing watches. We could keep it up right along, year after year, and do it right. But we got to hurry because of the situation with Jim."

"What are we going to do, then?"

"It ain't moral, and I wouldn't like it to get out, but there's only one way: we got to dig Jim out with the pick and shovel and *pretend* they're knives."

"Now you're talking!" I says. "I don't care shucks about the morality of it. When I start in to steal a nigger, I ain't particular how it's done, just so long as it *is* done. And I don't give a dead rat what the authorities thinks about it, neither."

So we switched to a pickax and shovel. We stuck to it about half an hour, which was as long as we could stand up, and we had a good-sized hole to show for it.

Next day, Tom stole six candles from the house. I hung around the nigger cabins, waited for a chance, and stole three tin plates. Tom said that three warn't enough, but I said nobody ever would see the plates that Jim throwed out because they'd fall in the weeds under the window-hole. We could fetch them and use them over again. That satisfied Tom.

That night, we went down the lightning rod a little after ten o'clock and took one of the candles along. We listened under the window-hole and heard Jim snoring.

We dug with the pick and shovel. In about two and a half hours, the job was done.

We crept in under Jim's bed and into the cabin. We lit our candle and stood over Jim awhile. He looked healthy and hearty. We woke him up gentle and gradual.

Jim was so glad to see us, he almost cried. He wanted us to find a chisel and cut the chain off his leg right away. He wanted to clear out without losing any more time.

But Tom set down and told Jim our plan. Tom said we could change it in a minute any time there was cause for alarm. He told Jim not to be afraid because we would see that he got away. He told Jim we'd smuggle in a rope-ladder pie and other things. Jim must be on the lookout and not let Nat see him open anything.

Jim couldn't see no sense in any of it, but he reckoned that Tom and me must know better than him 'cause we was white folks.

Jim had plenty of tobacco and corncob pipes, so we all had a good sociable time talking about old times. Then Tom and me crawled out through the window-hole and headed for the house.

Tom was in high spirits. He said it was the best fun he ever had in his life, and the most intellectural.

Chapter 21

At breakfast Mrs. Phelps was red and cross. She says to Mr. Phelps, "I've hunted high and low, and I can't find your white shirt. It was on the clothesline yesterday."

My heart fell down to my livers.

"The shirt ain't all that's gone, neither," Mrs. Phelps says. "Six candles is missing."

Just then the nigger woman steps into the passage and says, "Missus, dey's a sheet gone. It was on de clothesline yeste'day, but it ain't dere no more."

"A sheet gone, too!" Mrs. Phelps says.

Tom and me sure was glad when breakfast was over. That night we put the sheet back on the clothesline and stole one out of Mrs. Phelps's closet. We tore the sheet into strings and twisted them together until we had a lovely rope that you could've hung a person with.

The next day, we went to the rubbish pile in the backyard and found an old tin wash pan to bake the pie in. We stopped up the holes as well as we could and took the pan down to the cellar, where we stole enough flour to fill it. We cooked the pie away down in the woods. When we went to put the rope in, it was way too long, so we tore off an amount that would fit and throwed the rest away.

We told Nat that we'd bring the runaway nigger his food. We put three tin plates in the bottom of the food pan and put the pie in with Jim's other food. Jim opened the pie and hid the rope ladder in his bed. He scratched some marks on a tin plate and throwed it out the window-hole. Tom gave Jim the white shirt and piece of red chalk and told Jim he must write something on the shirt every day. Tom said he'd wrote a mournful message that Jim could copy. When Tom read it out loud, his voice trembled and he almost broke down: "Here a poor prisoner, abandoned by the world, went to his rest after thirty-seven years of solitary captivity."

Jim said he couldn't write that message or any other because he didn't know how to make letters.

"Well," Tom says, "you can make scribbles or something. That'll be good and mysterious, like a message in some secret language."

By the end of three weeks, everything was ready for Jim's escape. The bed leg was sawed in two, and Tom and me had ate up the sawdust, which give us a powerful stomachache.

Mr. Phelps had wrote a couple of times to the

plantation below New Orleans to come and get their runaway nigger. Of course, he hadn't got no answer because there warn't no such plantation. So he decided to advertise Jim in the St. Louis and New Orleans newspapers. When he mentioned the St. Louis ones, it give me the cold shivers because I see we hadn't no time to lose.

"Now for the anonymous letter," Tom says.

"What's that?" I says.

"A letter that isn't signed with your name. It'll be a letter warning Aunt Sally and Uncle Silas that something is up."

"Looky here, Tom. What do we want to warn them for?"

"Because they don't take notice of nothing at all. If we don't warn them, there won't be nobody to interfere with us. After all our hard work, this escape won't amount to nothing."

"Well, that's how I want it."

"Shucks!" he says and looks disgusted.

Tom wrote a letter and shoved it under the front door. It said, "Beware. Trouble is brewing. Keep a sharp lookout. Unknown Friend."

The next night, Tom drawed a picture of a skull and crossbones, and we stuck it on the front door. The night after that, we put a drawing of a coffin on the back door.

I ain't never seen a family in such a sweat. Mr. and Mrs. Phelps couldn't 've been more scared if the place had been full of ghosts behind everything, under the beds, and shivering through the air. Tom said he never seen a thing work more satisfactory.

The next day at supper, Mr. Phelps said they was going to have a nigger on watch at both doors all night.

That night, Tom went down the lightning rod to spy around. The nigger at the back door was asleep, so Tom stuck up a letter:

A desperate gang of cutthroats is going to steal your runaway nigger tomorrow night. They have been trying to scare you so that you will stay in the house and not bother them. I am one of the gang, but I am betraying the hellish plot because I got religion and wish to lead an honest life. The gang will sneak down from the north, along the fence, exactly at midnight. They will have a false key and will go to the nigger's cabin to get him. As soon as they get in, I will ba like a sheep. While they are getting the nigger's chain loose, lock them in. You can kill them at your leisure. Do everything just the way I am telling you. I do not wish any reward other than to know that I have done the right thing.

Unknown Friend

Chapter 22

Tom and me was feeling pretty good after breakfast. We brought a lunch, took my canoe, and went fishing on the river. We took a look at the raft and found her all right.

We got back late to supper and found Mr. and Mrs. Phelps all in a sweat and worry. They made us go right to bed the minute supper was done. They didn't tell us what the trouble was, but, of course, we knowed because we was the cause of it.

About half past eleven, Tom and me got up and heard voices downstairs. We sneaked downstairs and looked into the sitting room. There was a crowd! Fifteen farmers was setting around, all fidgety. Every one of them had a gun. I felt powerful sick.

Me and Tom stayed just outside the room, listening. Tom whispered, "Ain't it bully, Huck? If I could do it over again, I bet I could fetch two hundred men!" Some of the farmers was wanting to start right now and lay for that gang. They said it warn't but a few minutes to midnight. Others was trying to get them to hold on and wait for the sheep signal. Pretty soon one of them says, "I'm for going and getting in the cabin first—right now—and catching them when they come." I almost dropped.

Tom and me was upstairs in one second and down the lightning rod in another. We ran through the dark to the cabin. Jim was waiting and ready to go.

"I'll slide out and give the sheep signal," Tom says.

But we heard the tramp of men coming to the door and heard them begin to fumble with the padlock.

One man says, "I told you we'd be too soon. They haven't come yet. The door is locked. Why don't I lock some of you in the cabin? You can wait for them in the dark and kill them when they come. The rest of you, scatter around and listen for them."

So in they come. They couldn't see us in the dark and almost stepped on us while we was hustling to get under the bed. But we got under all right and out through the hole, swift but soft— Jim first, then me, then Tom, which was according to Tom's orders.

Now we was in the shed and heard trampings close by outside. We crept to the door. Tom stopped us there and put his eye to the crack. But it was so dark that he couldn't make nothing out. Tom whispered that he would listen for the steps to get further away. When he nudged us, Jim must glide out first and me next. So Tom set his ear to the crack and listened. There was steps scraping around out there all the time.

At last Tom nudged us, and we slid out— stooped down, not breathing, and not making the least noise. We sneaked towards the fence and got to it all right. Jim and me went over it, but Tom's pants caught on a splinter on the top rail. We heard steps coming, so Tom had to pull loose. That made the splinter snap. As Tom dropped alongside of Jim and me, somebody calls out, "Who's that? Answer, or I'll shoot!"

We didn't answer—just ran as fast as we could. There was a rush and a bang, bang, bang! Bullets whizzed around us.

We heard the men yell, "There they are! They're headed for the river! After them, men! Turn the dogs loose!"

Here they come, full tilt. We could hear *them* because they wore boots and yelled, but they couldn't hear *us*. We was in the path to the mill. When they got pretty close to us, we dodged into the bushes, let them go by, and dropped in behind them.

They'd had all the dogs shut up so that they wouldn't scare off the robbers. But by this time somebody had let the dogs loose. Here they come, making a racket. We stopped in our tracks 'til they catched up. When they see it warn't nobody but us, and no excitement to offer them, they only just said howdy and tore right ahead towards the shouting and clattering.

We whizzed along after them 'til we was nearly to the mill. Then we struck up through the bushes to where my canoe was tied. We hopped in and pulled for dear life towards the middle of the river. Then we struck out, easy and comfortable, for the island where the raft was. We could hear the men yelling at each other up and down the bank, 'til we was so far away that the sounds got dim and died out.

When we stepped onto the raft, I says, "Now, Jim, you're a free man again. I bet you won't ever be a slave no more."

"An' a mighty good job it was, too, Huck," Jim says.

We was all as glad as we could be. But Tom was the gladdest of all because he had a bullet in the calf of his leg.

When me and Jim heard that, we didn't feel nearly as happy as what we did before. The wound was bleeding and hurting Tom considerable, so we laid him in the wigwam and tore up a shirt to bandage him.

But Tom says, "Gimme the rags. I can do it myself. Don't stop now. Don't fool around here! Set her loose!"

But Jim and me started thinking and consulting. Jim says, "Dis is de way it look to me, Huck. If it was Miste' Tom dat was bein' set free, an' another boy was to get shot, would Miste' Tom say, 'Save me; never mind about a doctor to save *him*'? Would he say dat? You bet he wouldn't! Well den, is *I* goin' to say dat? No, sir. I ain't goin' to budge a step out o' dis place widdout a doctor. Not if it's forty year!"

I reckoned Jim would say what he did; I *knowed* he was white inside.

I told Tom I was going for a doctor. Tom raised a considerable row about it, but Jim and me stuck to it and wouldn't budge. Tom tried to crawl out and set the raft loose himself, but we stopped him.

When Tom sees me getting the canoe ready, he says, "Well, if you're bound to go, I'll tell you what to do when you get to the town. Blindfold the doctor tight and fast, and make him swear to be as silent as the grave. Put a purse full of gold in his hand. Then lead him all around the back alleys and everywheres in the dark. Then fetch him here in the canoe, in a roundabout way amongst the islands. Search him and take his chalk away from him, and don't give it back to him 'til you get him back to the town, or else he'll chalk this raft so that he can find it again. It's the way they all do."

I said I'd do what Tom said, and I left. Jim was to hide in the woods when he see the doctor coming, 'til the doctor was gone.

Chapter 23

I woke up the doctor. He was a kind-looking old man. I told him that my brother Sid and me was over on Spanish Island hunting yesterday afternoon, and we camped on a raft that we found. About midnight Sid must've kicked his gun while he was dreaming because it went off and shot him in the leg. I asked the doctor to go over and fix Sid's leg and not say nothing about it to anybody because we wanted to come home this evening and surprise the folks.

"Who is your folks?" he says.

"The Phelpses, down yonder."

"Oh." After a minute he says, "How'd you say your brother got shot?"

"He had a dream," I says, "and kicked his gun."

The doctor lit his lantern and got his saddle-bags, and we started. But when he seen the canoe, he didn't like the look of her. He said she was big enough for one but didn't look safe for two

I says, "Oh, you needn't be afeared, sir. She carried the three of us easy enough."

"What three?"

"Why, Sid and me and . . . the guns."

"Oh." He put his foot on the canoe and rocked her. He shook his head and said he reckoned he'd look around for a bigger one. But they was all locked and chained. So he took my canoe and said for me to wait 'til he come back, or maybe I better go down home and get them ready for the surprise if I wanted to.

I said I'd wait for him. I told him just how to find the raft. Then he started.

Pretty soon I struck an idea. I says to myself, "Suppose the doctor can't fix Tom's leg right away. Suppose it takes him three or four days. What are we going to do? Lay around there 'til he lets the cat out of the bag? No, sir. I know what I'll do. When he comes back, if he says he's got to go to the raft some more, I'll get down there, too, even if I have to swim. We'll take the doctor, tie him, keep him, and shove out down the river. When Tom's done with him, we'll give him money for helping us and let him get ashore."

I crept into a lumber pile to get some sleep. When I waked up, the sun was away up over my head! I shot out and went for the doctor's house. They told me he'd gone away during the night and warn't back yet.

"Well," I thinks, "that looks powerful bad for

Tom. I'll dig out for the island right off." So I hurried off. I turned the corner and nearly rammed my head into Mr. Phelps's stomach!

He says, "Tom! Where you been all this time?"

"I ain't been nowheres," I says. "Sid and me been hunting for the runaway nigger."

"Where did you go? Your aunt's been mighty uneasy."

"We're all right. We followed the men and dogs, but they outrun us, and we lost them. We thought we heard them on the water, so we got a canoe and took out after them and crossed over. But we couldn't find nothing of them, so we cruised upshore 'til we got tired out. We tied up the canoe and went to sleep. We never waked up 'til about an hour ago. Then we paddled over here to hear the news. Sid's at the post office to see what he can hear, and I'm branching out to get something for us to eat. Then we're going home."

So we went to the post office to get "Sid." Just as I suspicioned, he warn't there. Mr. Phelps got a letter out of the post office, and we waited for "Sid" a while longer.

Then Mr. Phelps says, "Come along. Let Sid foot it home, or canoe it, when he's done fooling around. We'll ride."

I couldn't get him to let me stay. He said there warn't no use in it and I must come along and let Aunt Sally know that "Sid" and me was all right.

When we got home, Mrs. Phelps was so glad to see me that she laughed and cried at the same time. She hugged me and give a licking that didn't amount to shucks. She said she'd do the same with "Sid" when he come.

The place was plumb full of farmers and their wives. They was there for lunch. And such a clatter a body never heard.

Old Mrs. Hotchkiss was the worst. Her tongue was going all the time. She says, "Well, Sister Phelps, I've looked over that cabin, an' I believe the nigger was crazy. The bed leg was sawed in two for no reason at all."

"An' there was a rope made out of rags, Sister Hotchkiss," old Mrs. Damrell says. "What, in the name o' goodness, could he ever want with *that*?"

"An' look at that shirt—every last inch of it covered over with secret African writing!" Mr. Marples says. "There must've been a houseful o' niggers helpin' him to do that. I'd lash them 'til . . ."

"People to help him, Brother Marples!" Mrs. Phelps cuts in. "I reckon you'd think so if you'd been in this house awhile. Why, they stole everything they could lay their hands on. They stole that shirt right off the clothesline. They stole flour and candles and a sheet. And now they slides right in under our noses and gets away with that nigger safe and sound, and that with sixteen men and twenty-two dogs right on their heels!" Suddenly she jumps up and says, "Mercy, it's almost night and Sid not come yet. What's become of that boy?"

I see my chance, so I skips up and says, "I'll run right up to town and get him."

"No, you won't," she says. "You'll stay right where you are. One's enough to be lost at one time. If he ain't here to supper, your uncle will go."

Well, he warn't there to supper, so right after supper Mr. Phelps went. He come back about ten o'clock a bit uneasy. He hadn't run across Tom's track. Mrs. Phelps was a good deal uneasy, but Mr. Phelps said there warn't no occasion to be. "Boys will be boys," he says. "You'll see this one turn up in the morning all safe and sound."

So Mrs. Phelps had to be satisfied. But she said that she'd set up for "Sid" awhile anyway and keep a light burning so he could see it.

When I went up to bed, she come up with me. She tucked me in and mothered me so good that I felt mean. I couldn't look her in the face. She set down on the bed and talked with me. She said what a splendid boy "Sid" was and kept talking about him. Every now and then, she asked me if I reckoned he could've got lost, hurt, or drownded. At this minute he might be laying somewheres suffering or dead, she said—and she not there to help him. Her tears dripped down silent, and I told her that Sid was all right and would be home in the morning, sure. She squeezed my hand and kissed me.

When she was going away, she looked down in my eyes steady and gentle and says, "The door ain't going to be locked, Tom, and there's the window and the lightning rod. But you'll be good, won't you? You won't go, for my sake?"

Lord knows, I wanted to go see about Tom and was all intending to go. But after that, I wouldn't 've went for kingdoms. I slept very restless because Mrs. Phelps and Tom both was on my mind. Twice I went down the lightning rod and slipped around front. I see Mrs. Phelps in the window, setting by her candle, with her eyes towards the road and tears in them. I wished that I could do something for her, but I couldn't do nothing except to swear that I wouldn't never do nothing to grieve her anymore. The third time I waked up, at dawn, and slid down, she was still there. Her candle was almost out. Her old gray head was resting on her hand, and she was asleep.

Chapter 24

Mr. Phelps was uptown again before breakfast, but he couldn't get no track of Tom. Mr. and Mrs. Phelps set at the table not saying anything and looking mournful. Their coffee got cold, and they didn't eat anything.

By and by, Mr. Phelps says to Mrs. Phelps, "Did I give you the letter?"

"What letter?"

"The one I got yesterday out of the post office."

"No, you didn't give me no letter."

"I must've forgot it." He rummaged in his pockets, took out the letter, and give it to her.

She says, "Why, it's from St. Petersburg! It's from Sis."

I figured a walk would do me good just then, but I couldn't stir.

Before Mrs. Phelps could break the letter open, she dropped it and run because she seen something. So did I. It was Tom Sawyer on a mattress;

that old doctor; Jim, with his hands tied behind him; and a lot of people.

I hid the letter behind the first thing that come handy and rushed out.

Mrs. Phelps flung herself at Tom, crying out, "Oh, he's dead!"

Tom turned his head a little and muttered something that showed he warn't in his right mind.

Mrs. Phelps flung up her hands. "Thank **God**, he's alive!" She snatched a kiss of Tom and flew for the house to get the bed ready. She scattered orders right and left at the niggers and everybody else, as fast as her tongue could go.

I followed the men to see what they was going to do with Jim. The doctor and Mr. Phelps followed Tom into the house. The men was very huffy. Some of them wanted to hang Jim as an example, so other niggers wouldn't be trying to run away like Jim done. They said he made a lot of trouble and kept the Phelpses scared almost to death for days and nights.

But others said, "Don't do it. He ain't our nigger. His owner will turn up and make us pay for him."

That cooled them down a little. The people that's the most anxious to hang a nigger always is the same people that's the least anxious to pay for him. They cussed Jim considerable and give him a cuff or two on the side of his head every so often.

Jim never said nothing. He never let on to know me.

They took Jim to the same cabin and chained him again—not to the bed leg this time but to a big staple drove into the bottom log. They chained both legs and his hands and said that he warn't to have nothing but bread and water to eat 'til his owner come or he was sold at auction. They filled up our hole and said a couple of farmers with guns must stand watch around the cabin every night.

They was cussing Jim when the old doctor come in. "Don't be no rougher on him than you're obliged to," he says. "He ain't a bad nigger. When I got to where I found the boy, I saw I couldn't cut the bullet out without some help. The boy warn't in no condition for me to leave and get help. He got worse and worse. After a time, he went out of his head and wouldn't let me come near him anymore. He said if I chalked the raft, he'd kill me—and no end of wild foolishness like that. I saw I couldn't do nothing at all with him. I says, 'I got to have help somehow.' The minute I says it, out crawls this nigger from some-wheres and says *he'll* help. And he done it, too, and done it very well.

"Of course, I judged he must be a runaway nigger. I had a couple of patients with the chills, and I wanted to run up to town and see them, but I didn't dare because the nigger might get away.

Then I'd be to blame. No skiff ever come close enough for me to hail. So I had to stay on that raft until daylight this morning. I never seen a nigger that was a better nurse or faithfuller. He was risking his freedom to help. He was all tired out, too. I liked the nigger for sacrificin' that way. I tell you, gentlemen, a nigger like that is worth a thousand dollars—and kind treatment.

"I had everything I needed, and the boy was doing as well there as he would've done at home—better maybe, because it was so quiet. But there I was with both of them on my hands, and there I had to stay 'til about dawn this morning. Then some men come by in a skiff. As good luck would have it, the nigger was setting with his head propped on his knees sound asleep. So I motioned them in quiet. Before he knowed what was happening, they slipped up on him, grabbed him, and tied him. We never had no trouble. By this time the boy was in a kind of flighty sleep. We hitched the raft to the men's skiff and towed her to shore. The nigger never made the least row. He never said a word. He ain't no bad nigger, gentlemen. That's what I think."

I was mighty thankful to the doctor for doing Jim that good turn. And I was glad it was according to my judgment of Jim. The first time I seen Jim, I thought he was a good man, with a good heart in him.

Somebody says, "Well, it sounds very good,

doctor, I'm obliged to say." Then they all agreed that Jim had acted very well and deserved some reward for that. I hoped they was going to say that Jim could have one or two of the chains took off because they was rotten heavy. Or that he could have meat and greens with his bread and water. But all they did was promise that they wouldn't cuss him no more. The men come out of the cabin and locked the door.

I judged I'd tell the Phelpses all the good things that the doctor said about Jim. But first I'd have to explain how I forgot to mention about "Sid" being shot.

Mrs. Phelps stuck to the sickroom all day and night. Every time I seen Mr. Phelps mooning around, I dodged him.

Next morning I heard that Tom was a good deal better. They said that Mrs. Phelps was gone to get a nap. So I slips into the sickroom. I reckoned that if I found Tom awake, we could come up with a story that would satisfy the Phelpses.

But he was sleeping very peaceful. He was pale, not red-cheeked the way he was when he come. I set down and waited for him to wake.

In about half an hour Mrs. Phelps comes gliding in. There I was up a stump again!

She motioned me to be still. She set down by me and begun to whisper. She said we could all be joyful now because the symptoms was first-rate. Tom had been sleeping a long time, and he was looking better and peacefuller all the time. Most likely, he'd wake up in his right mind.

So we set there watching. By and by, Tom stirred a bit and opened his eyes very natural. He takes a look and says, "Hello! Why, I'm at the house! How's that? Where's the raft?"

"It's all right," I says.

"How's Jim?"

"The same," I says, but I couldn't say it with any cheer.

"Good! Now we're all right! Did you tell Aunty?"

Mrs. Phelps chips in and says, "Tell me what, Sid?"

"The way the whole thing was done—how Tom and me set the runaway nigger free."

"Set the runaway . . . What is the child talking about? He's out of his head again!"

"No, I ain't. We *did* set him free. We laid out to do it, and we done it. We done it elegant, too." He rattled on and on, saying everything we done. Mrs. Phelps never stopped him. She just set and stared. "Why, Aunty, it cost us a power of work. You can't think half the fun that it was. We had to steal candles, and the sheet, and the shirt, and flour. And we had to draw the pictures and write the letters from the robbers, and get up and down the lightning rod, and dig the hole into the cabin, and make the rope ladder, and put it in a cooked pie, and . . ."

"Mercy sakes!"

"The men come before we was out of the cabin. We had to rush. They heard us and shot at us, and I got my share. We dodged out of the path and let them go by. When the dogs come, they warn't interested in us but went for the most noise. We got our canoe and made for the raft. We was all safe, and Jim was a free man. And we done it all by ourselves. Wasn't it bully, Aunty?"

"Well, I never heard the likes of it in all my born days! So it was *you* that's been making all this trouble. You turned everybody's wits clean inside out and scared us all almost to death. You little rascals! I've a good notion to take it out o' you this very minute. Here I've been, night after night, and . . . You just get well, you young scamp, and I'll tan both o' you! Don't you go meddling with that runaway nigger again. Thank goodness, we got him back, safe and sound. He's in that cabin again. He'll be on bread and water, and loaded down with chains, 'til he's claimed or sold!"

Tom rose up in bed. His eyes were hot. His nostrils opened and shut like gills. "You ain't got no right to shut him up!" he says. "Turn him loose! He ain't no slave. He's as free as any creature that walks this earth!"

"What do you mean?" Mrs. Phelps says.

"His name is Jim. I've knowed him all my life, and so has Tom. Old Miss Watson died two months ago. Before she died, she said she was ashamed that she ever was going to sell Jim down the river. She set him free in her will!"

"If he already was free, what on earth did you want to *set* him free for?"

"I wanted the adventure of it. I'd 've waded neck deep in blood to . . . Goodness alive! Aunt Polly!"

She was standing right there, just inside the door, looking as sweet and contented as an angel half full of pie.

Mrs. Phelps jumped for her, cried over her, and almost squeezed her to death.

I found a place under the bed and peeped out.

In a little while Tom's Aunt Polly shook herself loose and stood there looking across at Tom over her eyeglasses—kind of grinding him into the earth. "Yes, you better turn your head away. I would if I was you, Tom."

"*Tom?* I don't understand," Mrs. Phelps says. "Why, Tom is . . . Where's Tom?"

"You mean 'Where's Huck Finn?' Come out from under that bed, Huck Finn."

I did, but not feeling brash.

Mrs. Phelps was one of the most mixed-up-looking persons I ever seen—except for one, and that was Mr. Phelps when he come in and they told it all to *him*.

Tom's Aunt Polly told all about who I was.

I says, "I was in such a tight place that when Mrs. Phelps took me for Tom Sawyer, . . ."

Mrs. Phelps chipped in and says, "Call me Aunt Sally. I'm used to it now, and there ain't no need to change."

" . . . that when Aunt Sally took me for Tom Sawyer, I went along with it. There warn't no other way, and I knowed that Tom wouldn't mind. He'd think it was bully because it was mysterious and an adventure. And he *did* think that when he come. He pretended to be Sid and made things as soft for me as he could."

Tom's Aunt Polly said Tom was right about Miss Watson setting Jim free in her will.

So Tom had gone and took all that trouble to set a *free* nigger free. Until that minute and that talk, I couldn't understand how Tom could help a body set a nigger free.

Aunt Polly says to Mrs. Phelps, "When you wrote me that Tom and Sid had come all right and safe, I thinks to myself, 'What's Tom up to *this* time?' I wrote to you but didn't get any answer, so I thinks, 'Now I got to traipse all the way down the river, eleven hundred mile, and find out what's going on.'"

"Why, Sis, I never heard nothing from you," Mrs. Phelps says.

"I wrote you twice to ask you what you could mean by Sid being here."

"I never got the letters."

Aunt Polly turns around slow and severe. "Tom!"

"What?" he says.

"Don't you 'what' me, you fresh thing. Hand over them letters."

"They're in the trunk. They're just the same as when I got them out of the post office. I ain't looked into them. I ain't touched them. But I knowed they'd make trouble, so I . . ."

"Well, you do need skinning. There ain't no question about it." Then Aunt Polly says to Mrs. Phelps, "I wrote another one to tell you I was coming. I suppose he . . ."

"No, it come yesterday," Mrs. Phelps says. "I ain't read it yet."

Chapter 25

The first time I catched Tom private, I asked him, "What did you plan to do if the escape worked all right and we managed to set a nigger free that was *already* free?"

He said his plan was for us to take Jim down the river on the raft and have adventures plumb to the mouth of the river. Then he would tell Jim about his being free. He'd take Jim back up home on a steamboat, in style, and pay Jim for his lost time. He'd write word ahead that all the niggers around should meet the steamboat and waltz Jim into town with a torchlight procession and brass band. Jim would be a hero, and so would we.

But I reckoned things was about as good the way that they turned out.

We had Jim out of the chains in no time. When Aunt Polly and the Phelpses found out how Jim helped the doctor nurse Tom, they made a heap of fuss over him and fixed him up prime. They give him all that he wanted to eat, and a good time, and nothing to do.

We had Jim up to the sickroom and had a happy talk. Tom give Jim forty dollars for being such a patient prisoner and doing all the things that a prisoner should do, and Jim was pleased almost to death.

Then Tom says, "Let's all three of us slide out of here one of these nights, get Injun outfits, and go for howling adventures amongst the Injuns, out West, for a couple of weeks."

I says, "That suits me, but I ain't got no money to buy the outfit, and I reckon I couldn't get none from home because it's likely Pap's been back by now, got it all away from Judge Thatcher, and drunk it up."

"No, he ain't," Tom says. "It's all there yet: more than six thousand dollars. And your pap ain't ever been back since you was killed—at least, he hadn't been back when I come away."

Jim says, kind of solemn, "Your pap ain't comin' back no more, Huck."

I says, "Why, Jim?"

"Remember de house dat was floatin' down de river? Remember dere was a man in dere, covered up, an' I went in an' uncovered him and didn't let you come in? Well, you can git your money when you wants it because dat was your pap."

Tom's almost well now. He wears his bullet on a watch chain around his neck.

There ain't nothing more to write about, and I'm darn glad of it. If I'd knowed what trouble it is to make a book, I wouldn't 've tackled it. And I don't plan to do it ever again.

I reckon I have to head out West ahead of Tom because Mrs. Phelps wants to adopt me and civilize me, and I couldn't stand it. I been there before.

Afterword

ABOUT THE AUTHOR

"Mark Twain!" steamboat deckhands would call out to announce a safe water-depth of two (twain) fathoms. Samuel L. Clemens (1835–1910) was born in one river town (Florida, Missouri, on the Salt River) and grew up in another (Hannibal, Missouri, on the Mississippi). In 1863 he adopted the pen name Mark Twain, which reflected his love of the Mississippi River.

When Sam was a boy, the Mississippi was his region's main thoroughfare. He continually saw rafts, steamboats, skiffs, and canoes pass by on their way to unknown places and adventures. Sam disliked being indoors and frequently ran away from home—according to one biographer, "always in the direction of the river." Sam loved to swim in the Mississippi, play on its islands and shores, navigate it in a skiff, and sit at its edge for hours at a time. At age nine he stowed away on a steamboat headed south. (He soon was discovered and put ashore; relatives took him back to Hannibal.) At sixteen he swam across the Mississippi and back: a distance of at least two miles.

When his father died in 1847, Sam stopped going to school and became a printer's assistant. He was only twelve. From 1850 to 1857 he worked as a printer in various towns and cities. Then he moved to New Orleans and trained to become a Mississippi steamboat pilot. Sam learned the river's characteristics, in great detail, from New Orleans to St. Louis, a stretch of 1,200 miles. He became one of the best pilots on the river. In 1861 the Confederacy took his steamboat for use in the Civil War, ending his piloting career. After that, Sam would return to the Mississippi again and again in his writings, including his autobiographical *Life on the Mississippi* (1883). In *The Adventures of Huckleberry Finn* (1885), the river is such a strong presence that it can be thought of as one of the novel's main characters.

Perhaps the Mississippi meant so much to Sam because it represented freedom, in contrast to the slaveholding society in which he was raised. This is not to say that Sam found slavery repugnant or considered it morally wrong when he was a boy. He did not. "The local pulpit taught us that God approved [slavery], that it was a holy thing," he later would write. When Sam was growing up, a fourth of his town's population was enslaved. There always was at least one slave (either owned or leased) in the Clemens household and more than a dozen slaves at his uncle's farm, where Sam spent several summers. Anti-slavery speech and literature were outlawed. As a boy, Sam saw a mob attack an abolitionist, who was spared lynching only because a minister pleaded for his life on the grounds that he must be insane. Helping a slave to escape was a serious crime.

Slavery showed young Sam cruelties that must have disturbed him and aroused inner conflict, even if only subconsciously. He saw a slave killed over a trivial matter. His father sometimes whipped the Clemens' slave boy for merely being awkward or making a small mistake. Once, Sam's mother threatened the Clemens' young slave woman, Jennie, with a whip, and Jennie grabbed the whip from her hand. Furious, Sam's mother sent for her husband, who came home, bound Jennie by her wrists, and flogged her. As an adult, Sam "vividly" recalled seeing "a dozen black men and women chained together lying in a group on the pavement, waiting shipment to a Southern slave-market. They had the saddest faces I ever saw."

Another incident must have made a deep impression on Sam; decades later it would provide inspiration for *Huckleberry Finn*. Tom Blankenship, a poor white boy who was the model for Huck, was one of Sam's best friends. While hunting or fishing in a swamp, Tom's older brother, Ben, came across a runaway slave. The advertised reward for turning in the fugitive was $50—a considerable sum in those days, especially to someone as poor as Ben. But Ben didn't betray the runaway. Instead he helped him, for months, by bringing him food. When the fugitive's whereabouts were discovered, others went after the man. While attempting to escape, he drowned.

When the Civil War began, Sam's older brother, Orion—who was anti-slavery—sided with the Union. In fact, the Lincoln Administration appointed him Secretary of the new Territory of Nevada. In contrast, Sam, now in his twenties, joined the Confederate Army. But Sam's Confederate convictions must have been weak: he resigned from the army after only two weeks, accompanied Orion to Nevada, and briefly served as Orion's personal secretary.

Following an unsuccessful stint at California gold-mining, Sam became a professional writer (at first, for newspapers) and started using the name Mark Twain. His 1865 story "The Celebrated Jumping Frog of Calaveras County" brought him immediate fame. His first book, *Innocents Abroad* (1869), also was a huge success. Although Sam married and had children, he remained something of a "runaway," periodically spending time in other countries, where he gave readings and humorous lectures that were enormously popular.

Internationally renowned for his wisdom and wit, he wrote numerous essays, short stories, and novels, such as *The Adventures of Tom Sawyer* (1876) and *The Prince and the Pauper* (1882).

The theme of freedom versus oppression runs throughout Twain's work, most notably in *Huckleberry Finn*, which most critics consider Twain's greatest work and many consider the greatest American novel. In *Huckleberry Finn* the slaveholding society of Twain's youth embodies oppression, and the natural world, especially in the form of Twain's beloved Mississippi River, represents freedom.

ABOUT THE BOOK

Mark Twain wrote that in *Huckleberry Finn* "a sound heart and a deformed conscience come into collision and conscience suffers defeat." The "sound heart" and "deformed conscience" belong to the book's narrator and main character, Huck. His heart tells him to help Jim escape from slavery; his conscience tells him that helping a slave to escape is wrong. "I begun to get it through my head that Jim was almost free," Huck recalls. "And who was to blame for it? Me! I couldn't get that out of my conscience."

Huck is a white boy who has lived his whole life in the slaveholding South. His society has taught him that whites are superior to blacks and that slavery is a righteous institution. When Huck tells Sally Phelps that there's been a steamboat accident, she asks, "Anybody hurt?" "No, ma'am," Huck answers. "Killed a nigger." "Well, it's lucky," she says, "because sometimes people do get hurt." To whites of the slaveholding South, blacks weren't fully persons: *anybody* and *people* meant whites.

Huck thinks that Jim's intelligence must be unusual for a black man. "Well, he was right," Huck says of Jim. "He almost always was right. He had an uncommon level head for a nigger." After playing a trick on Jim that makes Jim feel foolish, Huck must overcome feelings of white superiority before he can apologize: "It was fifteen minutes before I could work myself up to go and humble myself to a nigger."

At times, Huck praises Jim for supposedly "white" qualities. For example, Jim mourns his separation from his wife and children, and Huck comments, "I believe he cared just as much for *his* people as white folks does for *theirs.*" Twain expects us to see the irony: Jim cares for his family much *more* than many whites care for theirs. Whereas Jim deeply loves his family, Huck's father feels no love at all for his son, whom he has continually exploited and abused. In fact, Jim is a much better father to Huck than Pap ever was. On the raft Jim often keeps watch during the night and then takes Huck's turn as well, allowing Huck to continue to sleep. Jim always treats Huck with kindness, affection, and protectiveness. When Tom is wounded, Jim and Huck agree that they must fetch a doctor rather than flee. "I reckoned Jim would say what he did," Huck remarks. "I *knowed* he was white inside." Again, Twain expects us to see the irony. White like the murderers on the sunken steamboat? White like the treacherous con men Blodgett and Bridgewater? Even though Tom himself has caused the crisis, Jim risks his freedom and life for Tom's sake. He stands in sharp contrast to the book's many base and cruel whites.

So does Huck, who believes that helping Jim is a sin for which he'll go to Hell: "I was so scared that I almost dropped in my tracks. I tried the best I could to soften it up for myself by saying that I was brung up wicked, so I warn't really to blame. But something inside of me kept saying, 'You could've gone to Sunday school. They would've learnt you that people that acts like *you* been acting about that nigger goes to everlasting fire.'" In one of the book's most poignant and powerful moments, Huck decides—"forever"—between rescuing Jim and (in his view) saving himself from eternal damnation. "All right, then," he declares, "I'll go to Hell."

How *does* Huck find the strength to go against his society's customs, laws, and beliefs? For one thing, he has not been as thoroughly brainwashed as most white children in his society. He *hasn't* gone to Sunday school—not often, at least. Until he lived with the Widow Douglas, he didn't attend school or church. Huck's father hasn't owned or leased slaves. In contrast, Tom *has* regularly attended school and church; his relatives *do* own slaves. Because of Tom's upbringing, Huck is astounded that "Tom Sawyer was going to help steal a nigger out of slavery. That was the thing that was too much for me. Here was a boy that was respectable and well brung up. . . . I couldn't understand it no way at all. It was outrageous." Whereas Huck wants to free Jim as quickly as possible, Tom makes cruel sport of Jim's captivity.

Huck is better able than Tom to feel the wrongness of Jim's enslavement because he is better able to *empathize* with Jim. Having been at the bottom of white society, Huck identifies with the underdog. Also, like Jim, Huck has been held captive: his father has kept him locked in a cabin, sometimes for days. He, too, has been abused: "Pap got too handy with his hickory switch. I was all over welts." He, too, is a runaway.

Jim and Huck have much in common, then. To some extent, both have been taught to accept their own victimization. Both Jim and Huck defer to Tom, their "social better," allowing him to tortuously prolong Jim's escape with pranks that considerably raise the danger level. Huck says of Tom's plan, "Jim couldn't see no sense in any of it," and readers, of course, agree with Jim. "But," Huck continues, Jim "reckoned that Tom and me must know better than him 'cause we was white folks." Who can read that without wincing? "He was risking his freedom to help," the doctor says of Jim. "He was all tired out, too. I liked the nigger for sacrificin' that way." Reading such statements, we easily feel anger even towards Jim. We want Jim to be *less* self-sacrificing, *less* humble, *less* forgiving. But we have to remember: Jim has spent his entire life in slavery. He constantly has been told that blacks are inferior to whites. Any refusal to submit to the wishes of whites has brought severe penalty. Is it any wonder, then, that Jim cannot fully recognize, and stand up for, his own worth?

Huck, however, always has sensed that worth: "The first time I seen Jim, I thought he was a good man, with a good heart in him." Huck can recognize Jim's goodness because he, too, has a "sound heart"—a heart that is stronger and larger at the story's end than at its beginning.

If you liked
The Adventures of Huckleberry Finn,
you might be interested in other
books in the Townsend Library.

THE ADVENTURES OF

TOM SAWYER

MARK TWAIN

TP THE TOWNSEND LIBRARY

Great STORIES OF SUSPENSE & ADVENTURE

- RIKKI-TIKKI-TAVI
- THE MONKEY'S PAW
- LEININGEN VERSUS THE ANTS
- THE LADY, OR THE TIGER?
- TO BUILD A FIRE
- THE MOST DANGEROUS GAME

TP THE TOWNSEND LIBRARY

(continued on following pages)

JONATHAN SWIFT

GULLIVER'S TRAVELS

TP THE TOWNSEND LIBRARY